DATE DUE

AUG 11 '06	
JUN 29 '07	
OCT 12 '07	
FEB JAN 24 12	
FEB 13 12	
JUN 1 13	
JUL 0 9 2014	

HERE
COMES
TROUBLE

HERE
COMES
TROUBLE

•

Kathy Carmichael

AVALON BOOKS
NEW YORK

PRINTED IN THE UNITED STATES OF AMERICA
ON ACID-FREE PAPER
BY HADDON CRAFTSMEN, BLOOMSBURG, PENNSYLVANIA

To my nieces, Kinsey Sue and Jordan Ashleah. You are the icing on the cupcake of my life!

To my talented editor, Erin Cartwright, who always knows exactly how to make my books even better.

To Trish Jensen, Cheryl Mansfield, Debby Mayne, Joyce Soule, and Alfie Thompson. Not only do you give me encouragement, you give me confidence to spread my wings.

And always and forever, my love to Ian, John, and Andrew—who love me despite pizza three times in a week and cabbage tasting like onions.

ACKNOWLEDGMENTS

My thanks to my sons, Andrew and Ian, who loaned me their names when I created the character of Ian Andrews. They are the light of my life and have never bombed me with water balloons.

Thanks to reviewers, Kathy Boswell and Janice Bennett, who made this book even more special.

The Trollz provided invaluable support and laughter during the writing of this book: Joanne Barnes, Carla "Lala" Bracale, Ali Cunliffe, Lynn Raye Harris, Avis Hester, Trish Jensen, Terry Kanago, Judy Miller, "Merry" Michelle Miller, Hannah Rowan, and RaeAnne Thayne.
To CB, the Troll deity: turn about is fair fodder.

Prologue

"So, the Ayes have it. Stella Goody and Quinlan Gregory will be married by Mother's Day." Cait Boswell's tone brooked no argument on the subject. "We'll start with making sure Quin is Stella's escort to their ten-year Littlemouth High School class reunion."

"Oh, no!" Debby Gregory's bracelets ceased their incessant clanking. She grimaced, then took a gulp of her high-protein smoothie, rumored to be fortified with something stronger. Her bracelets returned to their normal clatter. "I really don't think my son . . ."

"That's right, Debby. Don't think," said Cait with all the determination of a woman who'd found her mission in life. As the unofficial Ring

Leader and Sergeant-at-Arms of TROUBLE, she felt it was her sworn duty to keep them all in line. She steadily met the gaze of each of the five women cluttering her tidy living room. "Quin is the perfect answer."

The five ladies met weekly, ostensibly a reader's group, but more exactly as a cover for their true reason d'etre: gossip. They referred to themselves as TROUBLE, composed from the initials of their group, *The Readers Organization Uniting Book-loving Littlemouth Elites*. Everyone in town agreed that the epithet, TROUBLE, suited them ideally.

None of the five women, Cait, Debby, Prissy, Irma or Janice, was younger than fifty-five and they felt they'd earned the right to cause as much trouble as they considered amusing. If given a choice, most people would steer clear of them. But, between them, they headed up almost every volunteer league or civic position in the city.

There was no avoiding the interfering Trouble-makers.

"The reunion is a great idea," said Janice Smith, who resembled Mae West in not only looks but in outlook. She was always on the prowl.

"Isn't it romantic?" asked Miss Tipplemouse, clutching her bosom. Irma Tipplemouse, the only unmarried member of their group and their token spinster, had been somewhat scandalized, and then quietly delighted, when the denizens of their fair town began referring to them as the Troublemakers. "Imagine! Fate brought Quin home so he could be reunited with his one true love."

Cait laughed out loud. "That's an interesting fantasy, Irma, but really. They were best friends in grade school, not exactly lovers."

"Well, I think it's romantic." Irma Tipplemouse turned to Prissy Goody. "Don't you think it's romantic?"

"I don't think they even like each other," replied Prissy with a furrowed brow. "My daughter said she hated his guts."

"You know what they say about the fine line between love and hate." Debby tossed her head, upset by the idea someone didn't adore her son. The fact Quin had been considered the town's bad boy had never changed her high opinion of him.

Now, however, things had changed.

Quin Gregory had returned to town as the bad boy made good. As an investigative reporter, he wrote for one of the largest, if not *the* largest, weekly news magazines in the country. He was very good at his job.

Perhaps too good, considering how long it had been since he'd been home.

"Stella was six years old when she said that," said Cait. "Quin is the perfect man for her. The problem, as I see it, is whether she's interesting enough to get *his* attention."

Prissy gasped. "My daughter is a responsible young woman. Her job teaching biology at the high school—"

"Boorrring," said Janice, interrupting her.

"She owns her own home—"

"Boring." Again she was cut off, this time by Debby.

"Her column published in Good Gardens—"

"Not exactly titillating," drawled Cait. "Stella is full of spunk—but will Quin look below the surface? Men can be so superficial. She's a pretty little thing, but with his travels Quin is used to more glamorous women. Stella is perceptive, smart, and very amusing. But she's the girl he left at home."

"—Except for college, she's lived all her life in this town."

"For the most part, so have I," said Irma Tipplemouse.

That was enough to shut everyone up.

"Well," said Cait. "We'll just have to make her appear more interesting."

Prissy noticed the evil gleam in Cait's eye and asked cautiously, "What did you have in mind?"

By the time Debby called Quin and told him a

wee fib about her Harley misfiring and her need of a ride home, the others had worked out a game plan. When Quin arrived, each knew exactly what to do.

Chapter One

"Here comes trouble." Stella Goody glanced through the lace draperies lining her front windows. "It's about time you came home, Quinlan Gregory."

She'd just received a warning call from the neighborhood watch committee, telling her they thought Quin was on his way to see her. She could just make out a man some distance away, yet there was no doubt it was Quin. Her pulse raced as he sauntered down the sidewalk, closer to her front yard. A saunter that was unmistakably Quin's.

How had she forgotten how attractive he was? When had his childhood features taken hold in her memory, making her forget the handsome man he'd become?

6

Maybe now, thought Stella, nervously wiping her palms together, she'd have a chance to make amends for what she'd said to him the last time she'd seen him—ten years ago. She leaned closer, over pots of African violets thriving in the morning sunlight on the shelf in front of the window. The cool glass tickled her forehead as she pressed close.

Quin looked just the same, and yet, different.

A battered red pickup reared around the corner onto her street, spewing out black dust along with a series of backfires. Quin ducked and rolled to the ground.

What on earth?

Did he think someone was shooting at him?

Although, considering his job *and* his personality, probably many people wanted to shoot him. There'd been a number of times she'd have happily volunteered for the task.

As the truck disappeared from sight, she watched Quin stand and clutch his rib cage, while looking around sheepishly as if he was afraid someone had seen him behaving like an idiot.

She grinned. He'd always been an endearing idiot.

He began walking again, the sidewalk devoured by his stride. She smoothed her skirt, preparing to open the door in welcome to him. But he kept on walking.

Right past the walkway leading to her door!

Stella blew the hair out of her face.

As far as she could see, there wasn't any other reason for him to come this way except to see her. Maybe she should open the door and call out to him? No. That would come off as too desperate.

She should have realized some things never changed. Why expect Quin to be any different now? The rest of the town used to find him down-right infuriating, but she'd considered him exas-perating—and fun.

It wasn't as if he'd returned to Littlemouth to stay. If he'd stopped, she'd likely have set herself up for feeling abandoned by him again when he left. Yet, she was curious about him and hoped for an opportunity to reconcile their relationship after it had ended so abruptly ten years earlier.

As he passed her property, she noticed the little boy from across the street heading toward Quin. By all appearances, Ian Andrews was an adorable poppet of a five-year-old, with his red curls bounc-ing in the wind. It would be a sad day when his mother bowed to the requests of her husband to trim those curls, because they were stunning. In reality, though, Ian was Littlemouth's own version of a nuclear accident. Like a cyclone, the boy spun out of control, creating havoc in his path.

Stella wondered whether to warn Quin to keep his distance, but Ian carried a toy spaceman in his hands and was obviously having a great time talking to it.

The spaceman had been a bone of contention at the last neighborhood watch committee, with Mrs. Maplethorp complaining because of the loudness of the electronic noises it emitted. A compromise had been reached, however, and Ian had kept his toy. He was only allowed to play with it outdoors during daylight hours.

Quin was probably safe.

Stella covered her ears as the boy made a jab at the toy. A high-pitched squeal sounded.

Quin flinched. He had to keep reminding himself he wasn't in a war zone any more. He wasn't undercover in Kosovo. He wasn't in Kuwait, Iraq, Iran or any other number of dangerous places.

"You scared me, kid," he said. He was back home in Littlemouth, Kansas, the least dangerous and the corner of the world he'd once considered most boring. Now, however, things were different. "I don't suppose that was an air raid siren?"

"It was Super Spaceman," replied the boy as he studiously eyed Quin. "Super Spaceman had to let the powers of good know that Bad-ovo's forces have landed."

"Bad-ovo?" asked Quin as he squinted down at the child.

"He's the bad guy. Super Spaceman is the good

guy." The boy offered the toy to Quin. "Want to play with him?"

Quin gravely accepted the proffered spaceman and noted the series of multicolored buttons embedded in the toy's chest cavity. He punched a button and cringed as another shrill siren filled the air. "I'm going to have to get one of these. It's pretty cool."

"Yeah. He's the best. Only problem is, you can't play with him after dark. 'Dults around here," the boy nodded darkly toward the house they stood in front of, "don't like it."

"'Dults?"

"Mrs. Maplethorp. Anyone not a kid."

"My name's Quin. What's yours?"

"I'm Ian." He wiped his grubby hands on his jeans, then shook Quin's outstretched hand. "Want to come over and watch my Super Spaceman movie?"

"Sounds like fun, but I've got to head home now." He handed the toy back to Ian.

"Gotta tell your mom where you are, too?"

"Something like that," said Quin with a laugh. "It was nice meeting you." With a wave good-bye, Quin went back to his wandering.

As far as he could see, very little had changed in Littlemouth. His mother hadn't changed much either. And they said you couldn't go home.

Now that he was back, in his mother's case, he

wished she'd changed just a bit. Coming to her with banged-up ribs and a black eye, after a minor incident involving being tossed from a moving car by a group of bandits, hadn't been the best idea he'd ever had.

His mother was practically smothering him with attention, Quin thought, as he began the four block walk into town. He wasn't certain whether he might have been better off taking his chances with the angry bandits.

Retracing a path he'd traveled nearly every day of his childhood, on the other hand, proved a good idea. Sights and sounds he'd thrown off like bad habits returned in a crash to his senses. The funny rattle on the Thompson's heat pump. Chirping birds returning for the spring. A few trees opening tender green buds. A scent of daffodils in the cool spring breeze.

The Morrison's house now sported green shutters instead of blue. A new street light stood on the corner of Main and Henderson. Otherwise, he might be stepping directly into a page from his youth.

Nearing Main Street, he heard the bustle of cars, not like New York, but quiet. There was little noise to compete with the nesting birdsong.

He waved to Mr. Quick, the butcher, and looked in the pharmacy. He was tempted to enter the Five-and-Dime.

Right now, he needed to walk, look for changes, smell the smells, inhale the sights—of home.

Littlemouth hadn't changed. It was still the poky little town he'd longed to escape at the ripe age of eighteen. Was it possible to love a place and feel stronger knowing it existed, yet know deep down it wasn't the right place for him?

He craved the exotic vistas of foreign bazaars. The heady aroma of frangipani. The unique lilt of a Muslim in prayer.

Perhaps he was destined to forever be a wanderer, as he'd always thought of himself, with only a fond memory of home. The sameness of comparing your lawn to your neighbors, a typical nine-to-five job, the most dangerous encounter being whether you'd fall off the ladder while cleaning the gutters—none of it was for him.

Here he was, though, at home in this sleepy little hollow called Littlemouth, about at home as a rhinoceros in a department store. As soon as his boss gave him the all clear, Quin would be out of here and back to real life in a flash.

The only problem was that now he'd come home, part of him wanted to stay. He'd become used to being an outsider, the ugly American. The sense of belonging in Littlemouth was strong and it took him awhile to identify it because he hadn't experienced it in so long.

Littlemouth was one of the most beautiful cities

he'd seen in all of his travels. Sure, it didn't have skyscrapers or three-hundred-year-old buildings, but for him that wasn't what made a city great. It had heart—which was something he thought he might have misplaced years ago.

A sound called him from his thoughts. At first, he wasn't sure what the sound had been, but it disturbed his subconscious. He stood in place, listening.

Then he heard it: a whimpering and slight metallic rustle. He searched his surroundings, sought the source of the noise, then focused on a dumpster at the alley a few steps ahead of him. Walking forward to investigate, he heard more of a moan and he instantly identified it as a dog's cry.

Quin shoved up the heavy brown lid. There was no way the dog had gotten in there except by human hands.

Quin frowned.

Then he saw one of the largest dogs he'd ever set eyes on, making him think of Cerberus, the mythological Greek hellhound who guarded the entrance to Hades. Calling the animal hellhound might be more apt. He was a shorthaired mongrel, scarred, missing part of an ear, and half-starved. A black patch of fur covered one eye. Otherwise, his color was nondescript tan mixed with pink scar tissue. This brute had been in a lot of brawls.

"Hey, there, Tramp." His gaze caught sight of

blood. The animal's front two legs were badly gashed. The dog whimpered and his brown eyes pleaded with Quin for aid.

Quin sighed.

He had to go in. Quin propped the dumpster lid open with the metal brace to make sure it wouldn't snap closed. He pulled off his beloved leather bomber jacket, a high school graduation gift from his folks, and laid it neatly on some boxes near the dumpster. Then he tried to climb in, but his bruised ribs protested. A lot.

Quin looked around, found a wooden crate, then stood on it and managed to lower himself into the dumpster.

Phew.

His surroundings reeked of rotten trash, soured beer—and fear. "It's okay, Tramp," he softly said to the animal, who silenced immediately and looked at him out of those trusting brown eyes.

Quin could take him over to the vet, Doc Stephens, who'd patch him up and probably would know the owner. Trying not to appear threatening, he held out his hand. The dog licked it. "Suck up."

So far so good. Now to find a way to get him out. Quin made a move to inspect the animal's injuries—and the dog growled at him.

Quin had heard stories of people trying to help injured animals and being bitten for their efforts. He needed some way to protect himself.

Without hesitating for more than a second to mourn the loss, Quin grabbed the shoulder seam of his shirt and yanked. The sleeve came off and dangled from his wrist. The hellhound allowed him to bind his mouth. "Good boy."

The dog gave a timid wag to his stump of a tail. He was one ugly dog. Giving him a good pet, Quin said, "Hang on a little longer, Tramp. Trust me."

As he prepared to lift the animal, he heard the tip tap of high-heeled shoes on pavement heading their way. The steps halted in front of the dumpster.

Quin lifted himself up to see if help had arrived.

He froze. Then, without conscious thought, his hand snaked up to finger the acorn necklace he wore beneath his shirt. He looked into the one pair of innocent brown eyes he could never forget. Stella. Stella Goody with the same trusting brown eyes as the hellhound's.

She stared at him expressionlessly, opening and closing her mouth wordlessly. He'd pictured her in his mind countless times while on his travels, remembering her as the pesky little girl who managed to keep out of trouble while he always ended up neck-deep in it. He remembered the pact they'd made to never forget each other or their tree, and in minute detail he remembered the day Stella had given him the acorn she'd hollowed out, attached to a leather strap for him to wear. A necklace he never removed except to bathe.

He'd forgotten that she'd be all woman now. Little trace of his young friend remained, other than the tiny dimple-like scar perched just above soft inviting lips. A scar from the wound she'd received the day she slipped off the makeshift vine they'd used to swing from a large rock over the creek.

Quin wished he wasn't covered in garbage. He would have preferred to make a good impression on her.

Okay. So she was irrational. Stella couldn't believe she'd chased Quin down Littlemouth's Main Street just because he hadn't stopped at her house as she'd expected. It was certainly no reason to go tearing off after him.

So why had she bolted out the door and sprinted to catch up? Because she was certifiable. It was the only explanation.

When she'd heard Quin had come home, a quiver of anticipation had climbed up her brain stem. But watching him walk past her house had nearly done her in.

It was natural that she'd wanted to see him. However, they'd both grown up and grown apart. They were continents apart, not only in their outlook, but in what they wanted out of life. So why the heck had she chased him?

When Quin had disappeared down the alley, she'd hung back, not sure what to do.

Skulk. That's what she'd decided. Then she'd plastered herself against the corner of the brick building. When her ears hadn't picked up any indication of movement, she'd leaned around the edge of the building to peer into the alley.

Where had he gone?

At first she hadn't seen him in the alley's dim light, but heard what sounded like metal clanking against metal. She'd gone closer to investigate.

Suddenly, Quin's head emerged from a trash dumpster. She could smell the sour stench from where she stood. On his shoulder rested a banana peel and one of his shirt sleeves was missing.

Next, one of the ugliest dogs she'd ever laid eyes on popped up his sorry head. His snout had been tied closed by—so that was what had happened to Quin's shirt sleeve. What was he up to?

"Still hanging out with the wrong crowd, I see," said Stella, turning to leave. She felt foolish for blurting out old business.

"Wait," Quin called.

How many times as a teen had she ached for him to call out to her? She took a deep fortifying breath before shifting around to see what he wanted.

"I could use your help."

Stella raised her brow. Maybe she wasn't the crazy person around here. "You look like you could use a lot of help. Do you want the name of a good psychiatrist?"

"That's not exactly what I meant—but this dog's hurt and I can't get him out."

"Why not?"

"Banged-up ribs."

"Oh, yeah. I'd heard you came home needing some TLC."

"Where do I sign up for TLC?" he asked, wiggling his brows.

"I think your mother has that more than covered."

"You're right about that, but I can never get enough tenderness from attractive women."

"Still a charmer, I see."

"Think you could see your way into helping me—this hurt animal?"

Stella was a sucker for a sob story. Especially an injured animal's sob story. "What do you want me to do?"

Quin grinned. "You're not going to like it."

"Try me." His smile did things to her insides, things she'd rather not experience. It was too much like falling from a great height or riding an out of control roller coaster.

"You could start by removing your shoes. You might want to take off your stockings too."

"Quin, I'm not undressing for you—or for the dog."

"Very funny. I need you to climb in and help me get him out of here."

Stella whimpered. The last thing she wanted to do was climb in a stinky trash dumpster. "Are you sure you can't do it yourself? Or I can't help from out here?"

"Honestly, Stell, my ribs hurt. I jumped in to help him before thinking, and now I can't lift him without seeing stars. Please?"

"Misery loves company." Drat. Drat. Drat. The guy had always been able to talk her into doing things she didn't want to do. "Couldn't I go find someone else to help?"

"And leave this poor hurt animal in here that much longer?"

"Remove the banana peel and scooch over. I'm climbing in."

Quin shook the banana peel from his shoulder. He watched as Stella removed her shoes, revealing dainty toes. The dog must have wondered what was holding things up, because he'd removed his makeshift muzzle and barked, his tail wagging in friendly expectation. Obviously, the brute wasn't in as bad a shape as Quin had feared.

When it became apparent Stella wasn't going

anywhere fast, Quin said, "Don't worry. I'll catch you."

"What about your ribs?"

"I'll brace myself on these boxes."

He leaned against a box, then held out his arms to her. She swung herself into the dumpster faster than he'd expected and he caught her, letting out an audible gasp. Sure, his ribs hurt like the dickens—but what had him gasping wasn't pain.

Somehow, he'd caught Stella with one of his hands under her arm and the other came up clutching her hip. There was something about holding a handful of soft woman that did things to a man— like making him think of kissing her rather than concentrate on matters at hand.

Stella looked as surprised as he was. He heard the dog bark again and the sound of him scrambling around on the trash behind him, but it was nothing compared to the high-pitched buzz in his head.

"You can let go any time now," said Stella breathlessly.

"I don't think I can."

She started squirming and he figured if he didn't let her go, he'd steal a kiss for sure. He released her, easing her down into the dumpster. She looked flustered and a faint blush spread from her neck up to her face.

Her long lashes down turned, she wailed, "What do you have on your hands?"

Quin glanced at his palm and saw it was covered in black goop. When he looked back up at her, he laughed aloud.

Clearly imprinted on her skirt was the evidence of his groping: an unmistakable imprint of his hand covered her hip.

The shocked expression on her face was priceless.

Stella *was* still his favorite girl, although she was all woman now. There was something about Stella Goody and dumpster trash that made him feel all was right with the world. Nothing had changed in Littlemouth, Kansas. And he was darn happy about it.

After lending Stella his leather jacket to cover her stains, then dropping Tramp off at Doc Stephens', Quin headed for home and a shower. As he toweled off, his mother called and asked for a ride.

When he arrived at Cait's house, he saw it hadn't changed either. The big oak tree still shadowed the walkway, bringing to mind another oak tree he wanted to visit while he was home. His mother's motorcycle was parked beneath a pine tree and he wondered if he should take a look at it for her. Probably not, though. She knew more about motorcycle mechanics than he did.

Quin hadn't been inside Cait's house since he'd had a run-in with the school bully and had gone to her for first aid. While his mother was generally considered permissive, she was also known to overreact at the sight of injuries—particularly *his* injuries.

Cait had dutifully cleaned him up and scolded him about getting into fights.

Now he had to face TROUBLE en masse, a sobering thought.

Shortly after he knocked on the door, he found himself inside, being swarmed with hugs and kisses from his mother's friends. After carefully dodging Janice's too-moist kiss, he noted the group hadn't aged much except for a little extra steel in Cait's glare. She informed the others to give him a chance to breathe.

"It wouldn't feel like home if I didn't get hugs from my mom's friends," he replied with a smile. He hadn't realized how much he'd missed them all.

The aroma of Cait's famous shortbread made his stomach growl. "You didn't by any chance do some baking today?" he asked in the same tone he'd used as a boy whenever he smelled Cait's cookies. "That smell makes me mighty hungry and you know your baking is the best in Littlemouth."

"If you think I'm taken in by your sweet talk, you're sadly mistaken, Quinlan."

He gave her his best forlorn look and she cackled in response.

"You always did have too much charm for any one young man. Now you just follow me to the kitchen and we'll see if there's something for you in there." Cait gave the others a pointed stare and Quin wondered what it meant. He forgot the thought as soon as the swinging door into the kitchen opened to reveal a feast laid out on Cait's checkerboard tablecloth. Not only was there shortbread cut into neat triangles but also chocolate chip, peanut butter, and sugar cookies.

"I couldn't let you come home without making your favorite treats, could I, Quin?"

"Thank you, Mrs. Boswell. I've really missed your cookies—and you." He gave her a peck on the cheek.

She blushed as she bustled forward to get him a saucer. "Now, you help yourself, just like always. There's milk in the refrigerator."

As soon as she turned her back, he gobbled a couple cookies, then filled his plate and got a glass of milk. He knew something about Cait which he suspected few other people in Littlemouth knew: she was incredibly soft-hearted.

When he returned with plate and glass in hand to the living room, the ladies were peculiarly silent and he wondered if his mother had told them he was seriously ill instead of only a little bruised up.

Taking a seat on the maroon velvet rocker his mother indicated, he hoped he wouldn't spill his milk and stain it. Cait was extremely proud of her maroon velvet rockers.

"How are you doing, Miss Tipplemouse? Are things at the library okay?"

"I'll say," replied Miss Tipplemouse, who, ever since his voice had deepened, stopped being able to speak to him in sentences. She was extremely shy around men and sometimes it caused a few problems when an unaccompanied man came to the library looking for research help since the most answer any man could hope for from her was, "I'll say."

"Miss Tipplemouse made sure the library has a complete collection of your news articles, Quinlan," said Prissy Goody.

"What did you think of my article on the South American drug cartels, Miss Tipplemouse?" Quin's lips twitched, almost giving him away. Ever since middle school he'd been trying to trick her into talking.

"She couldn't stop discussing it for weeks, Quin," replied his mother, who was obviously onto his game.

Miss Tipplemouse nodded happily.

"I appreciate your interest," he said, then ate

another cookie to satisfy Cait, who appeared to be waiting for his reaction to her fine baking. "Mmm. I haven't had cookies this good in a long time."

Cait smiled but his mother gave him a cross look. "You'd think I didn't ever bake from the way you talk, Quin."

He grinned at her and ate another cookie. "You know what I think of your pies, Mom."

She smiled and he relaxed, knowing peace was restored.

"So, Quin, have you heard the latest Littlemouth gossip?" asked Janice in her vampish Mae West voice.

"About the new car dealership coming to town?"

"Oh, my," tittered Prissy. "That's old news."

"I seem to be out of the loop," Quin said. In the past, the women had been careful to curtail gossip in front of their children, as if said children weren't fully aware the reader's group was a front for rumor central. Evidently they considered him a grown-up now.

"Have you met anyone interesting since coming home?" asked Janice.

"I've only been home since yesterday. But I'm planning to go see Brendan McCade later today."

"Brendan has become a fine young man," replied Janice. "He makes a handsome deputy sheriff and wait until you see him in his uniform!

Makes my heart flutter. Most of the young women in town have tried to capture *that* one."

"Have you seen Stella?" asked Cait in an innocent voice which was enough to make Quin take notice. "Now, *she's* turned out to be an *interesting* young woman."

"I saw her in passing." He had to be careful here. The last thing he wanted to do was let them get wind of him groping her in a dumpster. "She's still teaching biology?"

Prissy nodded. "I suppose you heard about my daughter breaking off the engagement?"

"The engagement?" He was shocked, though hid it well. Somehow, he'd never thought about Stella marrying anyone. She really ought to have mentioned it before he'd begun fantasizing about kissing her. Besides, why hadn't his mother told him about Stella being engaged?

He scooted in his chair. Maybe things in Littlemouth had changed more than he'd thought.

"To James Dexter," added Cait.

"I hadn't heard anything about it." How could Stella think about marrying that stick in the mud? The kids hadn't nicknamed him Poindexter for nothing. Quin looked at his mother, hoping for a clue, but she had her gaze glued to her hands.

Janice jumped in, "I hope it won't embarrass you, Prissy, if I tell Quin?"

"I suppose it would be best coming from me, but I'm afraid I find it a bit too recent."

Janice leaned forward, as if to impart hush-hush information. "It all began when Stella took her Maid of Honor home to see her wedding dress."

"My daughter, Anne," chimed in Cait.

"You do know Stella inherited her grandmother's home over on Park Street, Quinlan?" asked Prissy.

"I'm glad to hear she got the house," he said as steadily as he could. "I always liked your mother. I was sorry to hear about her death."

"It's been several years, and while I miss her, I'm glad Stella has her own place."

"When Stella and Anne arrived," Janice said, drawing the attention back to herself, "James's car was parked in the driveway."

"So tragic," murmured Miss Tipplemouse, obviously much moved by the story and Quin wondered where it could be leading. When he'd seen her, Stella had looked like Stella, his childhood best friend and the prettiest girl in town. Of course, by the time they'd parted today, she'd looked a bit worse for wear—more like the dirtiest girl in town.

"Stella and Anne went upstairs to the guest room where Stella had hung her gown, but when they got there, the wedding veil was missing," Janice continued. "When they'd come in, they hadn't seen any sign of James, so now with both the veil *and* the groom missing, they became worried and began to search the place."

"Janice," said his mother. "I don't think—"

Cait gave her an extremely pointed look while Janice went on. "When they got to Stella's bedroom, what do you think they found?"

"She found Dexter with another woman?"

"No," cried Janice.

After a moment's hesitation, the ladies all laughed. Shrilly. What was so funny about that?

"If only that's what it had been," said Janice, melodramatically.

"What was it then?"

Janice beamed at him like he was a bright young man. He must have asked the right question. There was a breathless hush as each of the women became as motionless as a cobra about to strike.

"She found the groom trying on her wedding veil."

"Poindexter?!"

"Oh, my," moaned Miss Tipplemouse as she and the other ladies leaned forward in their seats. "Poor, poor Stella."

He had to admit that this certainly made her interesting—at least among the gossip set. As proud as Stella was, though, he knew she'd taken it hard. "Is she doing all right?"

"Oh, dear me, yes," answered his mother. "That

child has so many *interests*, what's a mere man when compared to them?"

"I'm glad to hear that." Poor Stella.

He checked Prissy's expression to see how she'd taken having her daughter's dirty laundry aired in public. She was gaping at Janice Smith as if she were some sort of alien being. Very strange and not at all the reaction he'd expected.

He shifted uncomfortably. Perhaps more had changed in Littlemouth than he'd first thought.

"You're aware, Quin, about the upcoming high school reunion?" asked Cait.

"I heard about it."

Prissy Goody leaned forward. "My daughter is too shy to ask you, but she hinted she'd like to go with you."

Stella was never too shy to speak up before, so he couldn't see why it would be a problem now. But maybe after her breakup she was feeling reluctant? "Thanks for the tip. I'll see what I can do."

Prissy gave him a big toothy grin and the other Troublemakers looked quite pleased with themselves. A tad too pleased.

Cait contained herself until she'd ushered Debby and Quin out the door. Then she turned to Janice and shrieked.

"I thought you were going to tell him she'd found him with another woman!"

"He expected that. You heard him. He wouldn't have found that at all interesting. So I ad-libbed a little. The story I told him was true." She giggled. "Except it took place in Muskogee and with other people. I read about it in the paper last week and it stuck with me."

Prissy stood with her hands on her hips. "I wish you hadn't told that zinger, Janice. My poor daughter would die of mortification if she heard such a story. I can't believe you did it."

Janice grinned broadly. "Well, I think it worked. Did you see the look on his face? He'll hightail it over to Stella's place within twenty-four hours and ask her to the reunion."

Prissy shook her head. "He probably thinks there's something wrong with her. My heavens, Janice, what will you think up next? You know there're such things as slander and libel."

"I sure hope we know what we're doing, ladies," Prissy continued, rising from her chair. "If we go too far, Quin may never come home again."

"Then we'll have to see that we don't make any mistakes," replied Cait in a voice of finality.

"We'll tell him about Stella being a bestselling author tomorrow," Miss Tipplemouse suggested gleefully. "I really like that one. With him being a famous journalist, I'm sure he'll find *that* interesting."

Chapter Two

When Stella pulled into her driveway after school the following day, her mother sat waiting for her in one of the two matching white wicker rockers adorning Stella's front porch.

Stella parked, grabbed her heavy satchel, then went to greet her mother. "You look nice today, Mom."

"Thank you, Stella." She eyed Stella's pastel blue suit and white blouse. "Perhaps we should go shopping next week? I think you could use an update."

"My clothes are fine for my lifestyle." Her mother wanted her to dress more like a student than a teacher. Stella unlocked the door and waited for her mom to go in, before using her foot to kick the door closed. "Come on in the kitchen and I'll make us both some iced tea."

"I can't stay long. I came to ask you a favor."

Stella dropped her things on the kitchen table, then went to the sink to fill the kettle with fresh water. "What do you need?"

"I ran into Millicent in town today."

"That snob?" Stella rolled her eyes. Millicent was the thorn in her mother's side. "Did she give you grief over Elise's engagement?"

"So, you know about it."

"Yeah, Elise called me yesterday and told me about her engagement. She warned me her mother might try to one-up you over it."

"It wouldn't have been so bad if she'd stopped there." Her mother bit her lip, then took a deep breath. "Stella, you have to help me out."

"I'm not going to run off and marry the first man I see, Mom, just to put Millicent in her place."

"Don't be silly. All I want is your promise."

Stella put the kettle on the stove and turned on the burner. "What's the promise?"

"That you won't go stag to the class reunion like you did to the prom. Is that asking so much?"

"I promise to take it into consideration."

"I'm sure one of my friends could find you a date if—"

"I'll find my own dates, thank you."

"But the reunion is less than two weeks away. At least promise that if anyone asks you, you'll agree to go with him."

"What if it's someone I don't like?"

Her mother frowned. "Well, you don't have to agree, if that's the case. But you have to be sure you don't like him."

"What if I think I'll be miserable if I go to the reunion with whomever this anonymous man is who asks me?"

"I don't want you miserable, Stella. I only want you to go to the reunion with a date."

Her mother meant well. Stella grinned, then gave her mom a kiss on the cheek. "I promise I'll keep it in mind when or if anyone asks me, Mom. But don't go around asking men to ask me. Got it?"

"I'd never do anything so heavy-handed, especially not without your permission."

"Good." Stella eyed her mother and wondered if her response had been too pat. "I *think* we understand each other."

"It's a mother's job to understand her daughter." Her mother smiled. "Now, I have to run and get your father's dinner before he goes to the town council meeting. I'll let myself out."

As her mother left the kitchen, Stella said, "Talk with you tomorrow."

"Don't forget to eat a good dinner with plenty

of vegetables," her mother called back as she left. Stella heard the door click closed, then reopen. "A man needs encouragement to ask a woman out. Don't forget to flirt a little."

The door closed again. Stella buried her face in her hands. Just what she needed right now: a nagging mother.

After first placing a tea bag in a mug, she quickly changed into an old baggy sweatshirt, jeans, and sneakers. If her mother saw her dressed like this, she'd do more than nag. She'd demand they do the shopping she'd threatened earlier.

Stella finished making her iced tea, grabbed her satchel filled with papers to grade, then headed out the back door. She loved her backyard filled with trees and shrubs, and now that spring had arrived, flowering bulbs. In another month or so, the wild-flower seeds she'd sown would sprout. But this time was exactly her favorite, when the garden was filled with potential and richness and tender shoots.

She slowly meandered through her yard, then made her way to the huge old oak tree situated in the middle of it. And to the tree house snuggled within its huge branches. She and Quin had built it over several summers when they were children. Her father had supervised, but they'd done the majority of the building themselves, including collecting materials for use.

Dangling from one of the branches was a home-made platform with pulley and rope attached, used for lifting items up into the tree. She placed her tea and satchel on it, then raised the platform.

After quickly climbing the rope ladder hanging from the middle of the tree house, she popped open the trapdoor in the floor and pulled herself inside. The tree house was about twelve feet square, but it had a snug wooden roof which she'd only had to patch once to keep the rain out, screened windows on all four sides, and the best view of Littlemouth in town.

Stella loved it up here, with the tree's leaves just starting to form. As long as weather permitted, she graded all her students' school papers in the tree house. It was also where she did all her major thinking. It felt safe, tucked up above the world.

After her broken engagement, she'd spent more and more time here, reinforcing the tree house supports, and making repairs. Besides her small desk and an old wooden rocking chair, she'd added a wicker divan, a bookshelf containing some of her favorite books, and a throw rug. She'd even done some decorating.

Stella loved sewing and had added a few touches to make the place feel homey. Working on the tree house had given her time to work out the complex emotions confusing her after breaking up with James.

It seemed all her friends had either married or moved away or both. James was reliable and responsible and had claimed to want all the things she wanted. She'd been lonely and when he'd asked her to marry him, she'd readily agreed, thinking it was wise to get moving on with her life. Thinking she'd finally get what she'd longed for.

What she wanted most in the world was exactly what her mother had, and what she'd enjoyed as a child. Stella wanted a family. A home and children of her own. And most of all, she wanted a husband to love and be loved by.

She'd attended college in Chicago. It was too large, too noisy, too busy. Upon graduation, she'd been happy to come home to a teaching job in Littlemouth, knowing she wanted a future in a cozy and warm small town.

In retrospect, she hadn't been in love with James, but she'd definitely loved her dream. When she'd found him in her bedroom closet, trying on her nicest pair of high-heeled shoes, she'd been shocked. When he'd asked her to let him try on her other shoes, she'd been devastated.

Now, months later, she could find the humor in the situation, but at the time . . .

She hadn't told anyone what had happened. Just told her mother and friends what she'd told James, that she was certain it couldn't work out. Her mother had tried to worm the story out of her, but Stella felt James's eccentricities were his private business. She'd been relieved when he left town.

The oak tree and its tree house had been her haven and her sanity. She'd had time, and the needed privacy, to sort through her feelings and realize she wouldn't fool herself again. She couldn't marry for anything less than real love.

Life had a way of going on and soon the rumor mill had run out of gossip about James and her. Now Littlemouth was buzzing with a new topic.

The bad boy had come home.

He'd looked every bit the bad boy when he'd strolled past her house. Later, when she'd seen Quin up close, she hadn't known quite what to think.

Her initial reaction had been how handsome and devil-may-care he looked, despite all evidence to the contrary. She'd wanted to hug him. She'd wanted to tell him to never leave again. She'd wanted him to hold her.

She was ridiculous.

It was pitifully obvious she lacked judgment when it came to the male of the species. So, she'd said the first thing springing to mind. She'd reminded him of their childhood argument about him ignoring her to hang out with the wrong crowd.

And he'd laughed at her.

She had to admit that she'd been pretty ridiculous, but his not having stopped at her house made her feel—abandoned. So she'd helped with the injured animal and gotten as far away from his devastating smile as possible.

Despite how everyone in town believed Quin had returned home as the bad boy made good, she couldn't quite believe he'd changed that much. He'd always been up to mischief. She couldn't help but wonder if he'd deliberately lured her into the dumpster simply to stain her clothing. She wouldn't put it past him.

Quin studied the baskets of ferns hanging on Stella's front porch while he waited for her to answer the door.

If Stella was too shy to ask him to the reunion, then he'd make it easy on her. Ten years before, she refused to attend the senior prom with him, and had then gone without a date, making it clear she preferred to go alone rather than in *his* company. Now he'd get a chance to show her his damaged ego didn't hold any grudges, that he'd grown up since then. Besides, going with her would be fun.

He rapped on the door again. Where was she? He paced back and forth on the slatted wood decking.

When she still didn't answer his knock, he decided to go around back. Even if she wasn't home, he wanted to see their old tree house.

Stella had done a lot of work on the yard. A small area was fenced off and staked out for a vegetable garden. Lots of seedlings had been planted. She'd always had an affinity for anything green. Too bad he hadn't been filled with chlorophyll instead of teenage hormones.

He looked up at the oak tree and couldn't believe his eyes. Not only was their tree house still there, it looked to be in even better shape than when they'd first built it. Walking beneath the structure, he noticed repairs had been made to it over the years. Amazing.

The trap door was open and he took it as an invitation to visit. He scaled the ladder and raised his head through the opening, wondering if there'd be cobwebs.

The first things he saw were flowery drapes over the window tops, then he spied a love seat with matching cushions and pillows with lace and frilly stuff. Glancing in the other direction, his gaze locked with Stella's.

He grinned.

" 'Welcome to my cobweb,' said the spider to the fly," she said.

"Thanks." He pulled himself the rest of the way into the tree house, then had to duck to avoid hitting his head on the roof. "This place has shrunk in my absence."

"I think you've grown, Quin," Stella said in an amused voice. "Quite a bit, in fact."

Still ducking his head, he wiggled his brows at her, then held out his arms and pivoted slowly. "You like?"

"I'm relieved you grew into those huge feet."

Quin looked down. "They're not so huge now."

"Oh, I don't know. They take up an awful lot of floor space." Stella smiled. "You look great."

"You're a sight for homesick eyes, yourself." Quin checked himself. "That was a lie."

"It was?"

"You're heart-stoppingly lovely, Stella. You haven't aged at all."

"Flatterer." Stella directed her gaze out the window. If only she were the type who could accept a temporary relationship. But she wasn't. She was constitutionally unable to engage in shallow flirting—she was an all-or-nothing type of person. Since Quin would be going on his way soon, it would be better for her peace of mind if she didn't start something he wouldn't be in town long enough to finish.

After a moment, she turned back and asked, "How are your ribs?"

"Not too bad." Quin began poking about the room, picked up one of the throw pillows, then checked out the books on the shelf. "The complete works of Jane Austen? You're still a romantic, then."

"Always was." Stella laughed, wondering why she didn't feel her space was invaded by Quin being in the tree house. No one had ever visited her here. In fact she'd discouraged it. Perhaps it was because she and Quin had shared so many childhood hours here, so many childish secrets. "But then, I never tried to hide the things I'm most interested in."

"What are you most interested in these days?"

"Oh, my job. I enjoy teaching the kids. I love gardening, sewing, cooking. And books, of course."

He looked at her skeptically. "That's it?"

"That's a lot."

"Haven't you ever longed for excitement?"

"All I've ever wanted were the small things life has to offer. A family, good friends, a rewarding job, a home that feels like a home."

He shrugged. "I want the same things."

"Only if they come with a dash of excitement and risk."

"Don't you get bored by the same routine day after day? Isn't it a little dull here after all these years?"

"I'll bet your routine isn't much different from mine. Like me, you probably get up and shower in the morning. But instead of heading off to browbeat kids into learning the rudiments of science, you knock heads with drug dealers or egomaniac monarchs in Third World countries, trying to get them to give you information."

"You have a point." Quin seated himself crossed-legged on the throw rug. "It's good to be home."

"Have you seen many of your old friends since being back?" she asked.

"Not really. I stopped by to see Brendan at the sheriff's office. It was a little surprising."

"Yeah, he's gone from Littlemouth's chief hellion to revered deputy sheriff."

"Littlemouth doesn't seem to have changed much."

"Only if you're looking at it from the outside, I suppose. Believe me, we've had our troubles and our highlights."

Quin got up and began pacing, at least as much as he could while stooping to avoid the ceiling. He lifted the brick they'd used to hide notes for each other and looked inside. "No mail, I see."

"I'm sure you get plenty of mail at home."

He shrugged again and it occurred to her what he reminded her of. A caged panther. He'd filled out since leaving home, muscle and tendon bulking out a frame that had once been too slender.

Each of his movements now was lithe, graceful in a masculine yet catlike way.

Stella felt sorry for him a moment. He must find Littlemouth confining.

He stilled. Tensed. "I've been doing a lot of thinking since I arrived."

"Don't overtax that brain of yours."

He caught her gaze. "When did we stop being best friends, Stell? I've missed our friendship. I've missed you."

She didn't know what to say. It was such old history, a childhood friendship that couldn't stand the test of time. "It was inevitable, I suppose. We grew up."

"You told me I was neglecting you for my other friends. Kids who were fast, running with the wrong crowd. Is that what did it?"

Stella shrugged. "I was jealous. I did feel neglected, left by the wayside. But we were kids, Quin, going through the normal pangs of growing up. I don't see how it could have been any different."

"You're right, of course. Have you had any dinner?"

Stella shook her head.

"Come out with me. I'm looking for an excuse to avoid another home-cooked meal. My mother is driving me nuts."

Stella laughed. "You intend to take up where

we left off, don't you? You used to say the same sort of thing as a kid."

"Some things never change. Now Mom thinks I'm an invalid. She keeps trying to force-feed me chicken soup. I swear, I'm beginning to sprout feathers. Let's go grab a hamburger."

"I'm not dressed to go out."

"You look great. Come on. Please?"

He'd always been able to talk her into anything, even when common sense told her better. "Let me change my shirt."

Quin waited outside while she changed. He'd come expressly to talk her into going to dinner with him and he was pleased she'd agreed. Ever since he'd seen her the day before, he hadn't been able to get her out of his mind.

She didn't seem broken-hearted over the break up with Dexter, but even if she was, would she reveal it? Stella had always been the quiet, contemplative type. He suspected she felt things more deeply than most people, certainly more deeply than he did.

He had a hard time believing someone as smart and inquisitive as Stella wanted to live forever in one place. She *had* to long for travel and new experiences.

It wasn't that Littlemouth was such a bad place.

It was a great small town. But surely she wanted to explore more of what the world had to offer?

She made him laugh not only at the world but at himself. It was a unique gift. Quin grinned. So she thought he was some kind of adventurer in search of the next lark. She wasn't far wrong, at least until recently.

He wasn't sure when he'd become dissatisfied, but it was there, lurking below his consciousness. He hadn't been concerned over it. His job kept him too busy for much self-examination.

Now he had this time off, though, it kept swimming closer and closer to the surface. Trust Stella to acknowledge it before he had.

"Okay," she said as she came outside holding his leather jacket. "Thanks for lending it to me."

The sight of her stopped his breath. Technically, he supposed, she wasn't beautiful, but to him she was the quintessential female. When she smiled, he wanted to strut like a peacock showing all his feathers.

The sight of her had always stopped his breath. She was so pretty in an understated way. She had the fairest complexion he'd ever seen. Just a few small freckles scattered over her nose, like saffron sprinkled on white rice. Her hair was the rich dark red his mother called auburn, but whenever he saw cherrywood it always made him think of her. Whenever he looked into her dark brown eyes, he knew he could trust her with his deepest secrets. In all his travels, he'd rarely seen eyes like hers.

She looked at him strangely when he didn't move to take the jacket. "Are you ready?"

Her words triggered all the wrong sorts of fantasies in his head. He was ready to kiss her. He was ready to feel her pressed into the curve of his arms. But she'd been the best friend he'd ever had. It would be stupid to risk what little remained of that friendship for something fleeting.

He accepted the jacket, then settled for brushing his lips against her forehead, breathing in her scent as if she were a flower bud he was afraid of bruising.

When he led her to his car, she walked ahead of him as if she, too, sensed something had changed.

Chapter Three

The Little Mouth Diner was considered one of Littlemouth's culinary masterpieces. In addition to its stock-in-trade hamburgers, it also offered such delicacies as fried chicken patties, fried corndogs, fried okra, fried corn fritters, fried onion rings, french fries, fried catfish on Sundays, and, in honor of the Lion's Club which met in the diner's back room, on Friday nights they offered fried popcorn shrimp. It was quite a happening place.

As usual on a Friday night, it was happening for Irma Tipplemouse and Janice Smith. They feasted on the dieter's special, consisting of a strange hodgepodge of food easily identified by a huge scoop of cottage cheese with a wedge of canned peach on top. Miss Tipplemouse came on Friday

47

nights to check out the Lion's Club members. Janice considered the diner her best source for fresh husbands.

"Have you gotten it yet, Irma?" asked Janice as she ogled a young man serving fries behind the restaurant counter.

"Not yet. But don't worry; I'll keep my part of our plan. There's plenty of time."

"I don't know about that."

"Surely Stella isn't what one could consider a fast girl?"

"She may not be, but I'd lay money on Quinlan being a *very* fast boy."

"I suppose you'd know."

Janice tittered. "I should hope so."

"I did try to buy it at the discount store this afternoon, but Mr. Harvest asked if I was out of toothpaste." Miss Tipplemouse gave a long, drawn-out sigh. "I bought three different brands and I'd just stocked up last month. I'll have to go back when his wife is working behind the counter."

"Try the bookstore. We're depending on you." Abruptly, Janice gasped. "Oh, I was right! Don't look yet, but guess who just came in?"

Miss Tipplemouse turned anyway, then quickly straightened. "Stella Goody and Quinlan Gregory. Well, I'll be. You were smack on the money, Janice."

"Let's just say, I know my young men," Janice bragged, then waved to the couple who immediately stopped by their table on their way in.

"Evening, ladies," said Quin.

"Nice to see you, Janice, Miss Tipplemouse," said Stella in a bright voice.

"How-de-doo," replied Janice.

"I'll say," replied Miss Tipplemouse.

Stella knew tongues would be wagging in the morning about her and Quin. When she'd seen her mother's friends, her first impulse had been to turn and exit the place but Quin had whispered, "Chicken." His comment hadn't applied to food.

He'd placed the palm of his hand on her back and shoved her in the door. If she were totally honest, she had to admit shoved wasn't exactly what he'd done, but it felt like it. The heat from his palm had burned all the way through her sweater, scorching her skin, propelling her into the restaurant faster than a sophomore shot out of a classroom at the ringing of the dismissal bell.

After parting from their mothers' friends, Quin led her to a booth along one wall. She didn't need to read a menu she knew by heart, but she studied it anyway. She was finding it increasingly difficult to keep her eyes off him.

He'd always been a study in contrasts, like a work of fine art. On the outside, he looked arrogant, proud, and powerful. Yet on the inside, he'd always been warm-hearted and sentimental. Was that part of him still there? After years on the road, facing unknown dangers, she expected he'd developed a shell of cynicism.

Could he be essentially the same person she'd once loved like a brother? If that was the case, why should his presence so disturb her now? She was aware of him, almost too aware. His once puppy large hands now looked rugged and manly. He never seemed at a loss for words or unable to charm. The way the pupils of his eyes had dilated just before he'd kissed her forehead earlier, she'd wondered if he intended to really kiss her. The idea alarmed her, yet at the same time made her stomach lurch in anticipation.

She had to be light-headed from hunger. Or maybe she was coming down with something. There was a flu bug going around at the high school last week.

Stella Goody had never once in her life gone swooning around, wanting to be kissed, and she wouldn't start now.

Would she?

"Your stories almost make me want to travel," said Stella as they left the Little Mouth Diner.

"I'd love to show you Malta. There's this little craft shop you'd go nuts in." Quin tucked her hand in his. "Want to walk home? It's too nice a night to waste. I can pick up my car later."

"Sounds nice." Her house was only three blocks away and his folks lived on the opposite side of town, so it wasn't such an odd suggestion. Although the night was a bit on the cool side, a huge moon hung down from a starlit sky, and Stella didn't feel the least bit chilled.

Neither of them spoke as they strolled down Main Street, but it was a comfortable silence. Companionable.

"Over there," Stella called out. "A shooting star."

Quin looked up.

In an instant, it was gone from sight. "For all your travels, I bet you've never seen a finer night sky than this."

"You've got me there." They turned the corner, leaving the street lights of Main Street behind. "I see Orion's Belt."

"Where?"

"See that big star over there?"

Stella couldn't find it. When Quin encircled her from behind, then pointed out the constellation, she couldn't concentrate on his directions. She was too intent on how it felt to have him so close.

There was nothing outwardly sensual about how he surrounded her. Yet, she responded—the top of her head seemed to curve into his neck. His shoulders were naturally wider than hers and served almost like a shield, leaving her breathless and feeling safe in the security of his arms.

She didn't want to go there. Her reaction to his nearness was bad enough. Her heart pounded. Her blood sang. And worst of all, a heavy longing filled her chest.

How could the friendly touch of a man she'd known since infancy do this to her?

She stepped out of his arms and began to walk again. Quin hesitated a moment before catching up. The silence between them became large and dissatisfying and she chastised herself for destroying their harmony.

They were back at her house only moments later. She could invite him in for coffee, but the idea made her feel awkward. She could tell Quin goodnight, but she wasn't certain she was ready for him to leave.

As they walked up the walkway to her front door, bright moonlight picked out slimy slug trails.

Slugs. She detested them. They destroyed her plants and seedlings. But they were almost a comfort now because she wouldn't have to end their evening since she could give him a task. Together, they had a job to do.

Her garden, with its plants she tended with such love and care, meant the world to her. A safe secure world where all things grew and thrived if given a chance. Whenever she saw those slug tracks, she felt like a Valkyrie, ready to wage war to defend her young.

Let the battle begin. "I'll be right back, Quin."

He looked at her peculiarly, but she didn't have time to worry about it. She had work to do.

Quin waited patiently for her return, perplexed about what she was up to. As far as he was concerned, it wasn't a bad thing. He liked surprises.

Within minutes she was back from the house with a salt shaker and a flashlight. She pushed the flashlight into his hand. "You can man the flashlight," she said. "I'll take the salt."

She started forward, but when he stayed where he was, she came back to him. "Follow their trails, Quin."

He had no inkling what she was talking about. "Whose trail?"

"The slugs. They're going to hurt my garden. You use the flashlight to follow the trail and I'll douse the blackguards with salt."

Quin shrugged. He didn't have anything better to do. Besides, Stella was cute. He'd stalked all sorts of vermin, but slugs would be a first.

"Keep the light down the length of the walk," she ordered. He had to hurry to keep up with her. Despite the fact that she was on all fours, she was after those critters at a fast clip.

This slug was a sneaky fellow because he kept circling back on himself. "I can't seem to find him."

The night seemed magical as they twisted in and out of the shrubbery and tromped through her yard. Occasionally his flashlight picked out brilliant red highlights in Stella's hair. Even in the dark, there was no missing the excitement shining in her eyes.

"Keep the light steady," Stella instructed.

Oops. It was hard concentrating on the slugs when so many other things in the flashlight's beam were more interesting. Stella, for instance.

Just then, the front porch light on the neighboring house switched on and the door opened. An elderly woman stepped out. "Stella Goody. Quinlan Gregory." The way she pronounced his name made it quite clear what she thought of him. "Is everything all right over there? Is that boy bothering you? He always was up to something."

"Everything's fine, Mrs. Maplethorp. I'm just on another slug hunt."

"Such nasty creatures. Go get 'em, Stella. If you need more salt, let me know. I'll be right here if you need me." The woman went back inside, but her light remained on.

"She hasn't changed her opinion of me." Quin laughed. "I believe she thinks I'm a worse threat than the slugs."

"She's just looking out for me, being neighborly." Stella went back to her task, giving him a nice view of her landscape. "Here's one! Hold the light steady while I douse him."

He guessed he had been directing the light to highlight her assets rather than the slug tracks again. As he stepped closer, shifting the light to beam in front of her, it dawned on him. He was having a wonderful time. It reminded him of when he'd first started out as a reporter for a small magazine. He'd been thrilled when he and a photographer had been sent to Burma to cover a story about a man-eating tiger. They'd stayed out too late, and had been caught in the bush. He'd never been so relieved as when they'd made it safely back to camp. The night had been much like this one.

"Why do you get to do the salt?" he asked.

"Because I know just the right amount to use."

The slug sort of writhed and Stella seemed very pleased by the fact. "You aren't going to eat it, are you?"

"No." She giggled. "It melts 'em, like the Wicked Witch of the West. If you use too much, though, it'll hurt the plants. So it's best I do it since I know how much to use."

"Seems like a lot of work. Do you do this often?" It seemed sort of a nutty thing to do. But watching her go after these slugs was something he wouldn't have missed for the world.

"It's become a ritual," she said, sprinkling on a little more salt. The slug didn't much seem to like it.

He laughed. She was the nuttiest woman he'd come across in a long time. He'd forgotten how much fun she'd always been, how much fun he'd always had with her. "Now what?"

"We go back to the sidewalk and start over again."

Moonlight lit up her gamine features. She was an elf or some other fairy creature, sent especially to enchant him. Quin couldn't resist anymore. He finally did what he'd wanted to do ever since seeing her again. He leaned forward and stole a kiss.

Maybe he'd intended it to be a friendly kiss, at least he hoped he had. But that's not what it turned out to be. Not when Stella grabbed him by the collar and dragged him closer. If he'd known as a teenager how well she kissed, she'd never have accused him of ignoring her.

What a kiss. It was sweet and poignant and womanly all at once. She tasted like vanilla and flowers and all things feminine and she was enticingly warm. How could one small bundle of woman make him feel so alive?

He wanted to keep kissing her, but he heard the sound of a door opening.

He cracked his eyes open. Mrs. Maplethorp.

Slowly pulling back from Stella, he whispered, "We shouldn't be doing this outside." He brushed a strand of her hair from her forehead.

Stella looked a bit dazed, but then she gave him a lazy smile and nodded.

He indicated Mrs. Maplethorp with his head. "We have an audience."

Stella turned to look. She groaned, then buried her face in her hands. "She's got her portable phone. She's probably giving a play by play to my mother."

He helped her to her feet, then they went to her front door, pausing just inside the open door. He kissed the tip of her nose. "I probably shouldn't come in."

"You're right. Nobody invited you."

"Of course I'm right."

"Did I ever tell you I hate it when you're right?"

He drew her back into his arms and kissed her again.

She felt just about perfect in his arms. Feeling pleased with himself, and a little smug, he gentled the kiss. "I should go now."

She leaned her head on his shoulder. "Yeah. I've still got papers to grade."

"I'll see you tomorrow?"

She nodded.

"Good. We can talk about what we want to do

after the reunion. I was thinking you might like to go to dinner, first, over in Topeka." She stiffened in his arms. "Then after the reunion, we could fly . . ."

She pulled herself away. "I might have known."

"What?" What was wrong?

"You arrogant, smug—slug." Her eyes shot daggers at him.

He'd seen that look before. Ten years ago, in fact. Quin gulped.

She put her hands on her hips. "You don't have any clue what you did, do you?"

There was no way he could answer without getting into further trouble, so he kept his silence.

"Did it ever once occur to you, you bigheaded lout, that I'd like to be asked? You told me I would be your date for the prom when we'd hardly talked at all in years. Now you come home after being away for a decade and do the same thing all over again."

Quin rubbed his face with his palms, palms still tingling from touching her only moments before. Had the Troublemakers gotten it wrong? Didn't she want to go the reunion with him?

"I wouldn't go to the reunion with you if you were the last man on earth."

"Don't say anything you'll regret later, Stella," he warned. Maybe Prissy had gotten it wrong; she was certainly wrong about the shy part. Surely she couldn't have gotten the reunion part wrong as well? "Your mother said—"

"Don't interrupt me. I'm trying to make a point."

He wouldn't laugh. It would only make things worse. The problem was that she was just as adorable angry as she was on a slug hunt.

"Just because I let you kiss me—"

"You *let* me kiss you? I thought there were two of us involved. *We* kissed each other."

"Let, kissed, it makes no difference. It was just a kiss. It didn't mean anything. You may be charming and handsome and, yes, intriguing, but that's all. If you'd asked me to go, maybe I'd have agreed."

Was that what this was about? Quin grinned. Now that he could handle. "Would you please do me the courtesy of going to the reunion as my date?"

"Too late, slug." She began to pepper him with a shower of salt.

Quin held up an arm to block the salt shower and realized he was knee-deep in figurative slug slime. "Honest, Stella, I was led to believe that you were expecting me to take you to the reunion."

"My mother?"

"The whole group of Troublemakers."

"I should have known." She'd suspected her

mother was up to something. "It's late, Quin. Time for you to go home."

"Okay, if I have to. But how about a goodnight kiss?"

She snorted.

It didn't seem like the sort of sound a woman would make before puckering up. He sighed. "I didn't think so."

"You were right for once." He heard her chuckle as she pushed him out the door, then closed it.

Quin stood there with his nose nearly touching the door for a few moments, totally clueless about how things had so quickly gone from perfect to wrong.

But then he smiled. It wasn't totally dire. She found him charming, handsome, and intriguing. He could work with that.

He turned, brushed the salt from his shoulders, and whistled as he strolled back to Main Street. Being home might prove to be an adventure. Based on Stella's kiss, he couldn't help but think she was as interested in him as he was in her.

Life hadn't been this fun in years. Everything about Stella appealed to him, made him grin ear-to-ear, and he was having a heck of a great time.

As he passed the house next door to Stella's, he called out, "Good night, Mrs. Maplethorp."

His only answer was the slam of a screen door as the porch light went out.

Chapter Four

The telephone lines in Littlemouth were burning like extra-hot jalapeno peppers. As usual, the Troublemakers were at the center of the maelstrom.

"Mrs. Maplethorp saw them with her own eyes . . ."

"He kissed her . . ."

"She grabbed him and kissed him . . ."

"They were making out like teenagers without a chaperone . . ."

"We did it . . ."

"A match made in heaven . . ."

"May will be a lovely time for a wedding . . ."

"You know what this means . . ."

"My son will stay in town!"

"My daughter will be married before Millicent's daughter!"

Stella's phone began ringing at 6:30 A.M. Deciding to let her machine pick it up, she groaned and buried her head under her pillow. Thanks to Quin, she hadn't fallen asleep until after three.

"I know you're home, Stella Elizabeth Goody." Her mother's voice was loud and clear over the answering machine speaker. "Pick up the phone."

Deciding to ignore her mother, Stella burrowed further under the covers.

"Call me." The answering machine disconnected the call.

Stella knew exactly what her mother wanted to talk about—Quin. She wasn't ready to talk about last night yet. She didn't even want to think about Quin.

Fifteen minutes later, the phone rang again. The caller didn't leave a message. After three other calls, one on top of the other, Stella gave up all hope of returning to sleep.

After a quick shower, she dressed and headed outside. She had some tomato seedlings ready for planting. Working in her garden was never a chore, and it also gave her a good excuse for not answering phone calls.

When she dug into the soil with a trowel, an image of Quin's cocky face appeared in front of her. Stella stabbed the earth. How could she have been dumb enough to kiss him? It wasn't as though she didn't know better.

She put a small plant into the hole, then moved onto the next spot. The soil fell away when she jabbed and twisted the trowel. It's a good thing Quin wasn't around or she'd be tempted to do the same to his smug slug face.

They'd seemed to get along so well last night. But a leopard didn't change his spots. He'd always been bossy and his success as a reporter probably reinforced it.

So why had she kissed him?

It's not as though he'd be staying in Little-mouth. Stella had to put a little dirt back into the hole because she'd been too exuberant with all that twisting and jabbing. She slipped in the next seed-ling.

Grabbing a rubber band from her jacket pocket, she pulled back her hair. A clump of dirt fell from her hair into her eyes. She rubbed her face with her arm, then leaned over to dig the next hole.

In a few short weeks, Quin would be long gone. Good riddance. She didn't need him confusing her, cluttering up her tree house and her life. And she sure as heck didn't need to spend any more time reliving how firm and secure his arms had felt around her or how gentle his kiss had been.

"There you are, Stella."

Her mother. Stella looked up. "Good morning."

"You're energetic this morning. I wondered why you hadn't answered my call."

"You called?" Stella hoped her face looked innocent enough.

Her mother silently eyed her for a moment and Stella wondered if she'd given herself away. "You're not wearing sun screen are you?"

"Guilty as charged."

"You've got a fine complexion now, but if you don't take the time to care for it, you'll regret it when you're my age." Her mother smiled. "I've come bearing gifts. I brought you some coffee cake."

Stella laid down her trowel, rose, and brushed off her knees. "I suppose you want coffee."

Her mother raised one brow. "That would be nice."

"That came out wrong, Mom." She hadn't intended to be rude, she simply didn't want to have the conversation her mother obviously wasn't about to let her avoid having. "Come inside and I'll get us some coffee."

When they entered her kitchen, Stella eyed the parcels in her Mom's arms and asked, "What else did you bring me?"

"Oh, this and that."

Stella rinsed her hands in the sink, then poured coffee into mugs. Would her mom take a hint? "I need to get those seedlings into the garden this morning."

As her mother removed her coat and settled into a seat at the table, Stella knew she wouldn't have that kind of luck. Not this morning. Not after Mrs. Maplethorp had told her mother about the kiss last night. Might as well get it over with. Moreover, she needed to point out the fact her mother had gone against Stella's wishes about the reunion.

"Do you need some help with making your pies for the fair tomorrow?"

"I've got the apples all cored and sliced." Stella shrugged. Her mother knew her methods so this was probably a conversational gambit. "I made the pastry ahead of time and it's thawing in the refrigerator. I'll bake them tonight."

"Your pies sold so well last year, it's good of you to offer a dozen of them this time. Miss Tipplemouse has been talking about a number of books she plans to order for the library with the money raised from the Trouble Tarts booth. Maybe this year, we'll beat the Ladies Auxiliary in the amount raised for charity."

The Friends of Littlemouth Spring Fair was a big event with various booths and games available in order to raise funds for several Littlemouth good causes. Everyone had fun and in return charities benefitted. Stella was looking forward to attending and it wasn't hard to prepare the pies for the

TROUBLE booth, especially since she did so much of it ahead of time.

"So, what brings you over so early this morning?" Stella placed saucers, silverware, and their mugs on the table.

"It's not that early. I've already been to the Ladies Auxiliary fundraiser. In fact, I got you something there."

Stella sat beside her mother. "Dare I hope it's one of Cait's birdhouses?" Cait made ornamental birdhouses as a hobby and Stella owned several.

Her mother nodded and handed her a plastic grocery bag. "I think you'll like this one."

Stella opened the bag and pushed the tissue aside. "It's darling." She placed the birdhouse on the table, then leaned forward and kissed her mother's cheek. "Thanks, Mom. As far as guilt offerings go, it's a good one."

"I'm glad you like it." Her mother cut the coffee cake and put a piece on each saucer. "I'm sure I don't know what you mean about it being a guilt offering, though."

"Quin told me you expected him to take me to the reunion."

"Why, I never said any such thing. I simply told him you were too shy to ask him."

"Mom." Stella shook her head. There was no point in belaboring the issue. When it came to audacity, her mother had an extra-large heaping.

The bag the birdhouse had come in was still in her hands and she fought an impulse to crumple it. When she tried to fold it, she realized it wasn't empty.

"More gifts?" She removed a rectangular gift box. "What's this?"

"Oh, it's for you." Her mother bit her lip. "Open it later."

Stella, of course, being her mother's daughter, did no such thing. She lifted the lid. Inside was one of those mini-books sold in grocery stores: *How to Lasso Your Cowboy.* "Mom—"

Her mother simply nodded.

Stella opened her mouth to explain that her relationship with Quin wasn't like that, but then she remembered the kiss from last night and firmly clamped her lips closed. No matter how much she insisted otherwise, her mother would never believe her. Glancing at the book's back cover, she noted it listed ways to get your fellow to propose. "I really don't think—"

"It's a mother's job to make sure her daughter is prepared."

"Mom, this isn't—"

"Let's not talk about it anymore, dear. We always did understand each other. Now, eat your cake."

* * *

The only problem with going to Doc Stephens' veterinary office, thought Quin as he stood at the reception desk, was it meant dealing with the receptionist, a.k.a. The Gargoyle. Just standing here, only a couple of feet in front of her, with that evil eye trained on him, was enough to make a grown man cringe.

The doc had kept Tramp overnight for observation, but had pronounced him fit and ready to go home. Quin was almost safe, all he had to do was pay for Tramp's care, and then he'd quickly get out of The Gargoyle's eyeball range.

She kept those narrowed eyes on him as he wrote out his check. "That an out of town or local check?"

"It's drawn on my bank in New York."

"Got any I.D.?"

Quin stopped writing. She really did have it in for him. "Is a driver's license enough I.D. for you? It's not as though you haven't known me since I was a kid or anything."

She humphed. "After your doings last night—"

Just then, Doc Stephens emerged from the back room, with Tramp on a leash. The dog barked a greeting at Quin.

"I'm sure Quin's good for it, Mrs. Gordon. Tramp's vouching for him."

She shrugged. "Takes one to know one."

When the doc offered Tramp's leash to him,

Quin wasn't sure why. Handing his check to The Gargoyle, he then took the leash.

"I should get the results on Tramp's blood work in a few days," said Doc Stephens, handing Quin a small green box. "You'll want to give him one of these pills once a month."

"There's some mistake," said Quin.

"No. These are heartworm pills." Doc Stephens clapped Quin on the back. "You'll do fine."

"When you said Tramp was ready to go home, I thought you meant home to his owner."

"Since you're footing the bill, I figured you *were* his owner, Quin. Tramp's a stray."

"I'm only going to be in town for a short while. Tramp can't go with me."

The Gargoyle made a strangling noise.

"Now, that *is* a problem," said Doc Stephens. "We can turn him over to animal control, but Tramp's not likely to be adopted in less than two weeks." Doc scratched his head. "After that, he'll be put down. Seems a waste."

"Don't you know anyone who wants a dog?"

"Can't say as I do. Mrs. Gordon, you know anyone who wants a fine dog like Tramp?"

She glanced at the dog, then rolled her eyes. Turning her back on them, she wheeled her chair to the other side of the reception area.

Quin stooped to pet Tramp, who wiggled his stumpy tail happily. There was no way he was turning such a great dog over to animal control. "Maybe Mom will keep him."

But things didn't go quite as well with his mother as Quin hoped. She'd taken one look at Tramp, then shrieked, "Not in my house!"

He wasn't sure what to do with the hellhound. He couldn't take him back where he'd found him. The dog trusted him. They'd walked into town together and Quin stopped in at the pet store to buy food. He also came away with a ball, throwing disk and rag bone. A healthy animal needs exercise.

His mom finally agreed to allow Tramp to stay in the yard until he could find another home for him. The problem was, who?

No, that wasn't the real problem. Instead of who, the problem was how. How best to convince Stella she wanted to be a mother?

Chapter Five

As soon as her mom left, Stella headed back to her garden, only to be constantly interrupted. Mrs. Maplethorp brought over a casserole, saying she'd made double by accident. Another neighbor brought cookies. Neither woman had wanted to come in, instead they were after gossip.

Stella wished she'd never heard of Quin. At the rate she was going, she'd never get her seedlings into the ground. When Cait came around the corner of her house, Stella decided it was time to throw in the trowel.

"If you want to know where Quin is this morning, I don't know," she announced, hoping to head off the endless questions she'd already fenced that morning.

71

"Quin's in the park playing with his mongrel, dear," replied Cait matter of factly, shifting a paper bag and a plastic wrapped plate of cookies. "I'm here to see you."

"Won't you please come in?" Stella led her into the kitchen.

Cait laid down her things on the kitchen table. "I hope you'll enjoy the cookies."

"Would you like something to drink?"

"No. I can't stay." She opened a paper sack on the table and pulled out a book. "This is for you. I've heard it's a best seller."

Stella glanced at the book. The title was written in screaming orange lettering against a navy background. *Man Hunting: How to Trap a Husband.*

Good heavens. First her own mother and now this. Evidently, they overestimated Quin's— charms. Or perhaps they were worried about her ability to attract a man? Come to think of it, they might be right. It was a depressing thought, and even more lowering was that they apparently believed she needed a man in order to find happiness.

Stella swallowed, not sure quite what to say. Good manners required she thank Cait. "I appreciate your thoughtfulness."

"If a thing is done, it's best done right."

Stella wondered if the pun had been deliberate as Cait gave her a quick peck on the cheek.

"I'd better run now," Cait said, gathering up her

belongings since her mission had evidently been accomplished. "Have to make it to the Ladies Auxiliary booth before they close."

Stella walked her to the front door. Someone was knocking as they arrived.

Cait said, "Oh, it's Mrs. Burnstein, I'd know that knock anywhere. Don't let her fluster you, dear."

During the next hour, Stella had no time to make it back outside. Visitor after visitor arrived, including Janice Smith, Quin's mother, and even the minister's wife. Finally, Stella left her front door ajar and kept the coffee pot set on brew.

She'd just been about to stick some of the casseroles and baked goods in the freezer when she heard Miss Tipplemouse knock timidly at the open door. "Stella?"

Stella, arms filled with plastic freezer containers, stepped to the hallway where she could see Miss Tipplemouse at the door. "Please come on in."

"Your door is open. Shall I close it behind me?"

"No point in it. I've had lots of visitors this morning."

"You've always been popular," said Miss Tipplemouse as she joined Stella in the kitchen. "I've brought you some coffee cake. Oh dear. I see you've already got some."

Stella tried not to snicker. *Got some* was truly

an understatement. She had enough cakes, cookies, and casseroles to feed the entire Littlemouth High School Senior Class after a hard day of conjugating verbs. Probably enough for the Junior and Sophomore class too. "Your cake has cherry filling, though, doesn't it?"

Miss Tipplemouse nodded.

"That's my favorite. Please have a seat and we can each have a slice. Would you like some coffee or tea?"

"Tea, please." Miss Tipplemouse clutched a shopping bag tightly in her hands.

Stella put all the food back on the counter beside the refrigerator. As she immersed the tea bag into a mug of hot water, Miss Tipplemouse said, "There's something I've been wishing to discuss with you."

"Yes?"

"I know you teach science—biology—at the school but . . ."

"Yes?"

"All those chemicals and, well, animals to be dissected . . ."

"Yes?"

"And you are careful to buckle your seatbelt when you drive, aren't you?"

"Yes." What on earth was Miss Tipplemouse trying to say?

"Then there's the matter of looking both ways at corners before crossing. Safety, I mean."

Stella nodded as she handed Miss Tipplemouse her tea, hoping she'd get a clue to the topic of discussion.

"Working at the library, I do have young people come in and ask for books on the subject."

"On the subject?"

"One can't be too cautious these days. For instance, I assume you use gloves at school?"

"Ah, gloves?"

"Yes, dear. When handling chemicals and such."

Stella was totally lost. She opened her mouth to try to clarify, but Miss Tipplemouse placed the shopping bag she'd been clutching onto the table in front of Stella.

"My, how I do run on, but I did promise the members of TROUBLE that I'd speak to you. I'm so glad we've had this conversation." Miss Tipplemouse arose. "You stay right where you are. I know my way to the door."

"Thank you," Stella called, but Miss Tipplemouse had already left. That had been one of the most confusing conversations she'd ever had, even with Miss Tipplemouse.

Pulling the rubber band from her hair, Stella shook her head. As she stood, her gaze landed on the bag Miss Tipplemouse had left. Maybe that would provide a clue to whatever she'd been try-ing to tell her.

She opened it and pulled out a book. Of course. *The Birds and the Bees: Worry-Free Dating and Marriage in the 21st Century.*

At first she didn't connect what Miss Tipple-mouse had been hinting with the book. Then it dawned on her what she'd meant. Safety. She ob-viously believed Stella needed a tried and true method for safely getting hitched. Stella didn't even want to *think* about Quin, yet the whole town had decided they were destined for marriage.

If only Quin didn't confuse her, leave her ach-ing for his touch. Now everyone in town evidently knew how she felt and it probably meant Quin did too. That wouldn't do, especially since she had absolutely no intention of acting on those feelings. She'd had enough of broken hearts.

"I visited Stella this morning," said Miss Tip-plemouse with a beaming smile, although no one could see it thanks to an overabundance of sofa pillows nearly blocking her from view. "Mission accomplished. I delivered the book to her."

In Debby Gregory's overcrowded front room, each of the other women seemed to freeze in time for a moment as their heads all swivelled to gaze at Miss Tipplemouse.

It was a peculiar assembly, with Troublemakers

scattered about a room filled to overflowing with anything and everything remotely resembling Native American decor. A bleached cow skull hung above the corner fireplace mantle, dream catchers covered each of the four windows, while above the windowsills, cloth resembling burlap draped down over deadwood rods. Running down the left side of the room was a staircase and the doweling had been decorated with feathers and woven tapestries. In addition to a Southwestern-styled sofa buried in gayly hued pillows, chairs covered in bearskin and Naugahyde were crammed into any available space.

Debby Gregory's great-great aunt, on her mother's side, had been full-blooded Comanche and Debby liked everyone to know through her decorating scheme. Her great-great aunt, on her mother's side, was probably writhing in the Great Burial Ground over said decor.

Of course, none of them had believed Irma Tipplemouse would follow through, but there was no way they'd admit it to each other. They'd privately supposed she'd be too embarrassed and so had taken the task on themselves.

Each of them became quite busy and none were able to meet each other's eyes. Miss Tipplemouse sighed happily. "It's so romantic."

They had gathered, hoping to receive an up-to-the-minute report on the developing romance directly from the source, Quin's mother. She had assured them that he was still at the park, cavorting with the creature he seemed to think was a dog.

"Mrs. Gordon called." Debby's expression was grim. "She said Quin is still intending to leave."

"What could have gone wrong?" said Mrs. Tipplemouse sadly.

"I'm disappointed in your son. Toying with my daughter's affections in a cavalier way—"

"From what I heard," said Debby, "Your daughter started it by grabbing him and kissing him—"

"Ladies," said Cait with a bit more vigor than necessary in such an overcrowded room.

They turned to face her.

"This is only a small setback," she continued. "From what I understand, it's Stella who's putting up the resistance. We'll continue as we planned, with, perhaps, a tiny addition."

"What did you have in mind?" asked Miss Tipplemouse.

"Our secret weapon."

A shocked silence lasted only seconds, then total chaos reigned.

"You don't mean—"

"You can't intend—"

"Not—"

"—Ian Andrews."

The name of the five-year-old terror struck fear

into the hearts of the entire populace of Little-mouth.

"If Quin were required to rescue Stella from the evil clutches of the little—*darling*, surely that would be romantic enough to turn the tide to our favor?"

"Let's go for it," said Prissy Goody. "How could my daughter resist?"

"Quin always enjoyed playing the hero," added Debby. "It's just the touch we need."

"Brilliant thinking," said Miss Tipplemouse. "Well done, Cait."

When Quin slammed into the house only seconds later, they each jumped as the door banged shut, then grabbed the book they planned to discuss when Quin arrived.

Debby stood. "Quin, dear, I hadn't expected you home quite so soon."

"Playing with Tramp wore me out." Quin took a seat on the stairs facing the living room where they were all gathered like witches in front of a cauldron—at least he supposed that thing in the middle of his mother's front room *was* a cauldron. It could be a wash pot, he supposed, although he was certain he'd never seen either turned into a coffee table before.

His mother automatically asked, "Are you feeling well? Do you want some chicken soup?"

"I'm fine, Mom. Thanks, but no soup." Quin

pointed to the book each of the Troublemakers held, entitled, *All Through the Day and Night*, by the bestselling novelist Constance Howard. "Is that Constance Howard's new book?"

Janice nodded, something akin to an evil nod if there was such a thing, leading him to assume Howard's latest must be even more titillating than her previous bestsellers.

Miss Tipplemouse clutched the book to her bosom and sighed melodramatically. "I'll say," she said.

"I've been looking forward to reading it," he added as further bait, but still they didn't take him up on it and clue him into the discussion.

Cait Boswell stood and smoothed the wrinkles from her skirt. "You know, Quin, there's something I've been meaning to tell you."

Prissy gasped. "You promised, Cait!"

Now *this* was getting good. Maybe there was some hot Littlemouth gossip to be had. Quin hitched up his pants legs.

"I most certainly did not promise. I agreed to take it into consideration—and I have." She smiled and all their faces became watchful. Too watchful.

Man, this was going to be good. "What have you meant to tell me, Cait?"

"You aren't the only famous writer in Littlemouth."

The entire room quieted enough to hear a pin not only drop but also roll. "I'm glad to hear that," he said. "I've had a problem bearing up under the pressure."

At that, his mother extended her copy of Howard's book to him. "Look at the author's picture."

With everyone's attention fixed on him, Quin realized for the first time that he might not like hearing what Cait had to say. What was going on? What did a writer of sensationalist fiction have to do with Littlemouth?

Pulling open the back cover, he skimmed the short author's biography which mentioned the man in the author's life, Doc Danger. Above the bio was a grainy black and white photograph. Like so many book cover photographs, the image wasn't clear and he had to do a double-take to get their meaning. Stella?

The woman pictured could certainly be mistaken for Stella, but they couldn't possibly be one and the same. Stella was sweet and the author was anything but. There was no way they could be the same person.

"This is Constance Howard," he said and couldn't help the tone of denial that crept into his words nor the question that followed. "This is Constance Howard?"

Prissy began fidgeting. His mother's bracelets started their jangling. Cait sat down with a Cheshire smile on her face while Miss Tipplemouse murmured something sounding like *romantic*. Janice tittered and said, "We're discussing the final scene. I contend that no one could write such a lurid scene without having actually experienced it. Your mother says it's purely drawn from the author's febrile imagination. As a writer yourself, what do you think?"

Chapter Six

Just when Stella thought things might have calmed down, she returned to her kitchen to continue straightening up. As she tossed the book Miss Tipplemouse had brought her into a shopping bag, she heard another knock at her door. She shoved it on the kitchen counter amid the pile of food ready to go in the freezer, then headed to the door.

Stella threw the door open. "You."

"Hi." Quin stood there, looking every bit as slug-like as the night before, irresistible grin and all.

"It's all your fault."

"What is?" he asked.

"The fact my house has turned into Grand Central Station."

"How's that my fault?"

Like she'd tell him about all the books? If he looked like a smug slug now, there was no telling how he'd look once his too-large male ego was complimented by a basement full of books on how to snare him. Then, once it dawned on him that the entire town had their sights on him, he'd flee faster than he'd ever fled before. "I don't want to talk about it."

He kept grinning. Why did that grin make her suspicious? Then she noticed his companion, the injured mongrel he'd been consorting with in the dumpster.

"Looks like Doc Stephens patched him up, but he appears to be hungry." Actually, now that she saw him on all fours, he looked more like the kind of animal children had nightmares about. Too bad she didn't keep dog biscuits on hand. Making sure he was well fed might be an act of self-preservation. "Do you suppose he likes coffee cake?"

"Can we come in?"

"Does he bite?"

"I don't think so." His tone didn't reassure her. "Is he housebroken?"

Quin wiggled his brow. "There's only one way to find out."

Stella didn't step back to let them in. She

couldn't even if she'd been inclined to. The dog looked evil and her body seemed to have perked as soon as she'd caught sight of Quin. She had to fight to keep from automatically tossing her hair. Why did he have to make her react this way? She felt like she was seventeen again and it *was* all his fault.

"He's a great dog. This morning I took him to the pet store and he stuck right with me."

"That's a good sign, I guess. But don't you think such a *great dog* has a worried owner?" She knew Quin's mother would never have such an animal as a pet. "Does his owner know he's hanging out with you?"

"Doc Stephens said Tramp's a stray."

"I guess we'll have to take his word for it." It wasn't too surprising. The animal would be the perfect companion for the phantom of the opera. With a mask to cover some of those scars, he might actually be presentable.

"That's why I came to see you."

"What?"

Taking advantage of her momentary distraction, Quin slipped past her and brought Tramp into the house. Darn.

She directed him to the kitchen where she put a couple of donuts and some coffee cake onto a saucer and gave it to the dog.

Quin stared intently at her. "Speaking of Docs, do you know someone called Doc Danger?"

"No. Why?"

"No reason."

Quin stood in the middle of her kitchen, so she hung out by the sink, as far from him as she could get. Her nerve endings were at a fever pitch. Down girl, down.

"It's going to be getting cold at night soon," said Quin, his eyes on the animal. "I've been thinking about it. That's probably how Tramp got into that dumpster to start with. He'd probably climbed in to get warm and the lid must have fallen and trapped him inside."

"I'm glad you found him."

"When I brought him home, Mom took one look at him and yelled, *Not in my house!* She agreed I could keep him in the yard until I found him a new home."

"There you go."

"I can't send him back to live in squalor, Stell."

"Squalor? Your backyard is hardly squalid."

"Yeah, but that's my point. He can't live in the dumpster and it's going to get cold."

"With summer on the way?" Now Stella knew what he was after and it wasn't pretty. Someday she'd planned to get a dog, something small and cute and pampered. Not a guardian of Hades. "Why do I always let you talk me into doing things I don't want to do? Do I have a sign saying 'patsy' on my backside?"

Quin gave her his come-hither smile again. "If it helps, you're a pretty patsy and your backside is Littlemouth's finest."

Stella rolled her eyes. She wasn't up to Quin flirting with her. To be honest, she was pretty annoyed with him. "If you're going to start talking like that, I'm going outside to play with my dog."

"My dog."

"I thought you just gave him to me."

"I didn't give him to you. I asked you to keep him." Quin couldn't believe Stella would jump to such a ridiculous conclusion about Tramp being *her* dog. That wasn't at all what he'd had in mind. It's just that when he thought of the notion of home, he thought of her.

"Same difference." She snatched up Tramp's ball, then opened the back door. "You're not sticking around for long, so it looks like Tramp belongs to me."

Quin followed Stella and the dog into the yard. Stella tossed the ball high into the air. Tramp ignored it.

Quin's brow wrinkled. Tramp had thoroughly enjoyed retrieving the ball earlier. What was wrong now?

"Go get it, Tramp."

The mutt scrambled to the ball, scooped it in his mouth, then offered the toy to Quin.

Quin patted his leg and whistled as he walked over to join Stella. The dog followed him. "Looks like he wants a mother *and* a father."

"I'm not ready for joint dog custody," Stella said with a toss of her head. "Besides, I'm still mad at you."

Amazing how Stella could look so attractive when her face was covered in dirt and her hair was all tangled. The urge to toss her over his shoulder and drag her off to his cave came over him. He tamped it down.

"You said it yourself. I can't keep him. Tramp needs a home. He'll adjust." Tramp settled himself at Quin's feet.

"Maybe he's trying to tell you he doesn't want to live with me?"

"Nah. I hadn't thought about it before, but it'll probably take him awhile to realize you're his new mommy."

"Let's just stick with owner." She walked over to join them. "You don't want a mommy, do you, Tramp?"

Quin watched as she leaned down to allow the dog to sniff her hand. He growled faintly. Stella quickly backed off.

"My fantasies of motherhood involve children, not ferocious beasts."

"Stop that, Tramp," ordered Quin.

The animal immediately silenced.

Stella crossed her arms and glared at both him and their dog.

Quin took a step toward her and Stella's eyes widened as she took a step away. He resisted an urge to wipe his sweaty palms on his jeans and took another step toward her. She took another step back. He dashed after her. Stella turned and ran.

Adrenaline pumped into his bloodstream, making his heart pound. He expected to react this way during the thrill of chasing down a lead or while undercover on a story.

He anticipated where she'd head next, and crisscrossed under the tree house, expecting to catch up with her. Stella compensated and ran the other way. Tramp got into the act and began to chase her along with Quin.

Littlemouth, Kansas, wasn't supposed to be exciting. Yet somehow Stella made the simplest things, like rushing around her back yard and arguing over a dog, feel—exhilarating.

He ran faster toward her, although he wasn't quite sure what he'd do once he caught her. He wasn't about to let that deter him. Tramp neared her, then grabbed her jeans cuff in his jaws, tripping her.

Quin was just in time to catch her as she fell into his arms. He was going to have to give that dog a treat. Then Tramp grabbed his cuff, sending Quin, arms full of woman, sprawling. He cushioned their fall as best he could, shutting his eyes when they made contact with hard ground.

A stab of pain shot through him as he landed, jarring the same body parts as had been bruised after his run-in with the bandits.

Wow. His body lie crushed beneath some substantial weight. Stella was a lot heavier than he'd thought. Something warm and moist brushed his face. She must like he-man antics. Quin opened his eyes, ready to do some serious kissing.

Stella was lying in his arms, he could feel her there, but Tramp was on top of both of them, drooling on Quin. "No treat for *you*, mutt."

"Do you think you can get him off us?" asked Stella with a laugh in her voice. "I think your hip bruised me, but thanks for taking most of the fall."

Quin gave Tramp a small push and the dog reluctantly backed off. "Are you okay?"

Stella hopped up. "I'm fine." As she brushed herself off, Quin noticed Tramp standing between them. Then Quin's attention fixed on Stella's face. He wanted to kiss her. He was homesick and Stella was home.

With great intent, he reached for her. Tramp evidently decided enough was enough though, because he placed himself squarely between them and began to pull on Quin's jeans leg. But this time Quin was prepared and managed to fend off the animal.

Tramp, however, was a very determined dog. He scampered directly to the seedlings Stella had been in the process of planting and began to dig.

Stella yelled as a shower of soil volcanoed into the air. Quin yelled, "Stop that," but Tramp paid no attention. He was on those plants with the determination of a terrier after his rat.

Quin ran over and grabbed Tramp's collar, momentarily halting the animal's destruction of Stella's beloved garden. "No!" he shouted.

Stella joined them and moaned softly. "My babies. He murdered my babies. I brought them up from seeds. It took weeks."

Quin couldn't bear to see her like this. While trying to keep a firm hold on Tramp's collar, he used his toe to tamp down a few of the survivors. Glaring at the animal, he said, "You did this on purpose, didn't you?"

Tramp lowered his head but couldn't quite manage to look contrite.

"I'm ashamed of you, mutt." Quin turned to Stella. "I suppose this means you won't keep him after all?"

"The damage isn't all that bad, Quin," she said, obviously trying to make the best of a bad situation. Quin felt horrible.

"Let's take him inside where he can't wreak

more havoc," Stella suggested. "I'll train him to stay out of the garden later."

"Good thinking."

"Besides," Stella added as she sashayed through the back door, "you need to wash off some of that mud."

"No matter how much I got into, it couldn't equal what you've had all over your face since I got here."

"What?" Stella ran to check. "Why didn't you say anything?"

Quin bit back a laugh. He wouldn't laugh. No way. Latching the screen door after Tramp came in, he went over to the sink and dampened a cloth to clean off the dog's paws.

Stella called out, probably from her bedroom. "I'm taking a quick shower and I'll be right out."

Quin answered, "We'll be fine. I'll get Tramp acquainted with his new home."

Determined not to think about Stella, he looked for things to keep his mind occupied. Tramp sat at his feet and stared at him. The animal must be hungry again.

Quin went over to where Stella had mounds of goodies beside the refrigerator. Opening one box, he pulled out a donut. Tramp stood up on two legs and begged.

What a smart dog. Quin gave him the treat.

Next, he opened a sack but inside it wasn't the

cookies he'd expected. Pulling out the book, he read the title, but couldn't quite keep a pleased smile off his face.

"Stella must like us, old boy," he said to Tramp who barked for another treat. Quin shuffled around in the pile of goodies and pulled out another book on dating.

She must like him a lot more than he'd thought. Maybe she did want to go to the reunion with him. Unless—

What if she was using the books to help her catch some other guy?

Quin sighed.

Tramp quickly gulped down the cookie Quin offered him, then they both sat to wait for Stella. Within minutes, she came into the kitchen, wearing a fresh T-shirt and jeans. She smelled of dusting powder, soap, and roses, a heady mixture for Quin, who'd become used to women wearing heavy scents. Even with her hair still wet from the shower and without a lick of makeup, she looked positively delicious and exactly like his favorite sort of dessert.

"I can't believe you didn't tell me I was covered in mud, Quin," Stella complained as she entered the kitchen. She wondered why he was eyeing her so intently. When he arose from his chair at the table, she began to feel like a stalked animal as he walked toward her.

Rubbing her hands together nervously, she evaded him and moved to the refrigerator. "I've got pies to bake for the fair tomorrow."

"Can I help?" he asked, coming up behind her.

Stella jerked away and swung open the refrigerator door, careful to wedge herself inside rather than be trapped by Quin. "Haven't you heard the saying, 'Too many cooks spoil the pie?' "

Pulling out a plastic bag filled with apple slices, she darted a look at him. He leaned on the counter between her and the sink, with his arms crossed and another slug leer on his face.

Grabbing the salt shaker, she said, "Don't force me to use this. I've got pies to bake, Quin."

He continued with that leer and she could tell he was hoping for another kiss. She didn't want to get started smooching with him again. Getting involved with him would be ridiculous, especially since she knew better. She simply wasn't the kind of woman who could settle for anything less than a real relationship. Why wouldn't he take a hint and leave? "Isn't it about time for you to be going somewhere?"

"I've got nothing better to do." He reached to remove the salt shaker from her hands and like a fool, she was the one who almost melted—from the tingle of his touch.

"Nothing better than standing around and getting in my way, you mean?" She had to get him out of her kitchen, her house, her life before she did something she'd regret for the rest of her life. There was no doubt that if she allowed herself to get too involved with him he'd break her heart.

Chapter Seven

J ust as Stella was about to tell Quin to go home, there was a frantic knock at her front door.

"I wonder who that could be," she said as she went to answer it. Opening the door, she found Terri Andrews with her son in tow.

"I'm so glad you're home. Your mother told me you would help me out." Terri urged Ian inside, but didn't come in herself.

"What's wrong, Terri?"

"An emergency meeting has been called to discuss the fireworks for the fair. I've got to go, but I can't bring Ian with me. Supper is on the stove and his bed time is in an hour."

Stella gulped. The child had terrorized his last three babysitters. But that was beside the point because by the time she opened her mouth to tell Terri she couldn't watch Ian, his mother had dashed off.

Stella called out, "But I have pies to bake!"

Terri either ignored or didn't hear her and continued on her way.

Stella gaped at Ian. What was she going to do now? She had to bake the pies for the booth tomorrow. As she closed the front door, Quin joined them in the entry area.

"Hey, Ian," he said, then asked Stella, "What's up?"

"Terri just dropped him off for me to babysit him. She didn't wait to hear that I've got to stay here and bake pies. Do you think you could run over to his house and turn off the stove? She said supper was cooking."

"No problem. Why don't I watch Ian while you work on the pies?"

"Quin, you don't know what you're getting yourself into."

"Sure I do." He ruffled Ian's curls. "Ian and I are great friends, aren't we, pal?"

"Yeah," replied the boy. "We can watch the Super Spaceman movie."

"See?"

Stella saw that she didn't have much choice. Since Quin wasn't a real babysitter, maybe the child would behave. They seemed to get along all right. "Thanks, Quin. That would be a great help."

"Come on, Ian. Let's allow Stella to get to her pies." He leaned forward and brushed his lips across her cheek.

She placed her fingertips over the spot he'd kissed. As they turned to leave, she called Quin back. "Whatever you do, don't play hide and seek with him."

Quin nodded and rushed after Ian who had already started on his way home.

Stella didn't much like sending Quin into disaster, but he was a grown man. He'd chased war criminals. Surely he could handle a five-year-old boy.

An hour later, all was not well at the Andrews' house. Quin stood in the basement, lit only by a single bulb in the middle of the room, hoping to see some sign of Ian.

"I told you, no hide and seek."

The only answer was a childish giggle.

Quin turned in that direction. He'd been in the middle of clearing up their dinner dishes when Ian had dashed to the basement door and declared that Quin couldn't find him, then the boy rushed down the stairs.

Quin put his hands on his hips. "Come out now."

Silence. Where was the kid?

He heard a slithering noise and hoped it was Ian rather than rats. Then he realized the sound came from the basement steps. Before he could reach them, he saw Ian running up the steps to the door.

Quin chased after him, but Ian was too quick. When Quin reached the top of the stairs, the basement door shut in his face and he heard the sickening sound of the lock turning.

Grabbing the knob, he twisted, but the door wouldn't budge. Then the light went out.

"Turn that back on!" he called.

"You can't get me," cried Ian gleefully, but he didn't switch the light back on.

"Open the door!"

"I'm getting a cookie," replied Ian, his voice tapering off as he evidently walked away.

Quin sighed. This must have been what Stella had meant about not playing hide and seek with Ian. If she'd explained, he wouldn't be in this fix. Slowly lowering himself to the basement steps, he took a seat and wondered how long it would be before Ian's mother came home.

Long minutes passed. He seemed to be sitting there forever. The enforced solitude began to grate on his nerves. Quin didn't like thinking about his motives in the best of times, and this was far from the best.

Maybe life had become too easy for him. Maybe

he was off his game entirely. Perhaps that explained how not only the bandits but also a little kid could get the best of him.

The only thing he was sure of was that going back to life as it was, chasing bad guys and writing about them, didn't hold much appeal. He loved the excitement, but going from battlefield to battlefield had become depressing. Right now, all he wanted was to get out of the dank basement, then go sit at Stella's kitchen table and watch her bake pies. In fact, he couldn't think of a better way to spend the rest of his life.

He wouldn't mind catching up with Ian too. As if thinking of the hoodlum conjured him up, just then Quin heard the sound of a window opening.

"Are you still in there?" asked the boy.

"Still here. Can you turn on the light now?"

"No, 'cause you'll find me."

Quin's eyes had become accustomed to the dark and he made out the image of the boy's face peering in a small window near the basement ceiling. Cautiously, and as quietly as possible, Quin descended the stairs, making good use of the stair rail on his way down. He toe-heeled to the window, hoping Ian wouldn't hear or see him.

As he neared, he saw the window wasn't large enough for him to get out that way. But maybe he could talk the kid into setting him free? "What about that Super Spaceman movie? I sure would like to see it."

"I've seen it lots already." Ian laughed, then threw something at Quin.

The something landed with a splat on Quin's face. Cold liquid dripped down his face. A water balloon? "Stop that and let me out of here."

"No way," said Ian, tossing another missile Quin's way.

Quin dodged it, but Ian hit him with the third balloon he threw. It hit Quin below the belt, and water seeped down Quin's legs.

He couldn't believe he was locked in some basement and having water balloons thrown at him. It was something out of whacked-out night-mares.

Another balloon made a direct hit on his head.

Quin had enough. With a quick stride, he reached the window and extended an arm to grab the boy.

Ian was too fast for him and had evidently prac-ticed his next maneuver. Within seconds, the boy directed a huge blast of cold water at Quin from the garden hose, completely drenching him.

Quin retreated toward the steps, hopefully out of hose rang. "Don't you think your mother will be upset when she comes home?"

"Maybe." The boy's voice trailed on the word, as if he was considering things. "Maybe she'll take away dessert for a week. That's what she did the last time."

"The last time you had a babysitter?"

"Yeah."

"Well, I'm not a babysitter." Quin fought to keep his temper in check. "Look, Ian. It's cold and dark down here. Don't you think you could come and let me out? That way, your mother might never find out."

"Since you're not a sitter, maybe she won't be mad."

"Or maybe she'll be more upset since I'm a guest?"

"Maybe I won't tell her you're down here."

"I think she'll find out when she hears me knocking."

"Maybe I'll tell her you're a burglar."

"Ian. Let. Me. Out."

The child blasted another current of water into the basement, then said, "I'm tired. I'm going to bed."

"Wait, Ian. Let me out and I'll read you a bed time story."

Quin listened, but there was no answer. The boy had wandered off and Quin could only hope that the child would be okay without adult supervision because there wasn't much he could do from down here.

After several attempts yelling for help through

the window without any luck, Quin then tried to read his watch, but there wasn't enough light. Returning to the basement stairs, he took a seat and prepared to wait for Ian's mother to come home.

He could only hope that word about his being trapped in a basement and pelted with water balloons wouldn't get out. Considering the Littlemouth grapevine, he figured the likelihood of keeping it quiet was minuscule. The most he could likely hope for was not catching pneumonia.

Chapter Eight

Once Quin and Ian left, Stella had gone right to work with her pie-baking after starting a cozy fire in her hearth. As she worked, Tramp behaved like a gentleman and stayed out of her way.

However, every time any sound could be heard from outside the house, he was up on his feet and at the front door with his tail eagerly wagging as if he expected Quin to return at any second. As if he believed *his* master wouldn't leave him here alone with Stella for long, no way.

"You probably think he's coming back for you."

He twisted his head, as if to say, *Of course he's returning for me. No way would a fabulous master like Quin leave me behind.*

Poor brute. If Stella wasn't careful how she handled herself around Quin, she'd delude herself into believing the same notion. He'd left Littlemouth and her behind ten years before and things weren't any different now.

She didn't have time to waste with fantasies. She kept working on the pies.

The next time she checked the clock, three hours had passed since Quin had left and she'd just finished baking eight pies. They were cooling on the kitchen table while four more baked in the oven. Stella glanced out her kitchen window toward the Andrews' home and was surprised to see all the lights on in the house.

She picked up the phone and quickly dialed the number. No answer. Something must be wrong. Surely Quin wouldn't have played hide and seek after she'd warned him not to?

Tramp came with her as she dashed out the back door and she locked him in the yard before heading for the Andrews' house. As she approached, she heard the sound of the hose running. Her heart sank. It appeared that Quin had received the same basement water torture as previous babysitters.

She quickly shut it off, then headed to the back door and let herself inside. She had no doubt about what had happened. Like most men, Quin had problems following directions—he'd played hide and seek with Ian.

As she headed toward the basement door, she

grabbed a couple of clean white towels out of the laundry room.

"Quin?" she called.

He didn't answer. Her fingers fumbled at the door lock, but at last she got it to turn. The basement was dark and she quickly switched on the light. There, in a huddled wet mass, she saw Quin asleep at the bottom of the stairs.

"Quin."

He sat up and rubbed his eyes, then smiled at her. "You've come to save me!"

"I don't have a white charger, but I've got white towels." Stella handed them to him as he reached the doorway.

"How did you know to come?"

"I saw the house all lit up and knew something had to be wrong."

"Thanks for the towels. It might be spring, but it's cold in the basement."

Just then, they heard the sound of Terri's car pulling into the driveway. "Good, she's home. Come back to my place and I'll make you something warm to drink and toss your clothes in my dryer."

"Sounds good. Can I watch you make pies too?"

His voice still sounded drowsy with sleep and she wondered if he'd been dreaming about the pies. He was making a manly attempt to disguise the chattering of his teeth. "Whatever you want."

Terri came in and Stella quickly explained what had happened. They all went to check on Ian, who looked like an angel as he soundly slept in his bed.

"I don't know what to do with that boy," Terri said as they walked to the door.

"Can I lock him in the basement and throw water balloons at him?" asked Quin.

"He didn't!"

"He did." Quin grinned.

"Don't tempt me," said Terri with a smile.

"As a favor, I'd appreciate it if his punishment is something more important to him than dessert."

"You got it. Thanks for not being angry."

"Right now I'm more cold than anything else."

"Come on, Quin," said Stella. "Let's get back to my place and get you something dry to wear."

They quickly said goodbye, then walked to Stella's. Tramp greeted them with a happy bark as they entered the back yard.

When they came through the back door, Stella said, "Stay right here. Don't move."

"Don't worry. I couldn't, even if I wanted to."

Stella dashed up the stairs and grabbed her bathrobe. It was the only thing in her house that had any hope of fitting around him. Maybe if she got him out of his wet clothes and poured some hot coffee into him, he'd feel better.

She ran back downstairs. "Go to the bathroom,

strip, and put this on. I'll stick your clothes in the dryer."

"Stella . . ."

"What?"

"Why are you trying to get me out of my clothes?"

Stella snickered. "You think I have designs on your virtue?"

"Don't you?"

"You wish." First pushing the robe in his arms, she shoved him into the bathroom and closed the door. "Hand me your wet things and put on that robe."

A few moments later, the bathroom door opened a crack. "Can I come out now?"

"Are you decent?"

"I'm always decent."

"Have you put on the robe?"

"It's got flowers on it."

"Quin!"

"Stella, have you noticed there's lace on it? You can't honestly expect me to . . ."

"Put on the darn robe!"

The door opened a little further and Stella threw her hands over her face to block the view of what she was certain would be seventy-two inches of partially clothed man.

"You can put your hands down."

"You're wearing the robe?"

She heard Quin give a long-suffering sigh and decided to risk it. He'd wrapped the robe carefully around his body and tied it with a neat bow.

He looked hilarious in her robe, like one of those old forties movies where the leading man dressed in women's attire and camped it up. She bit her lip to keep from laughing.

"If you laugh, I'm taking it off."

Fighting off temptation, she quickly said, "Let's get you settled by the fire so you can warm up."

She rushed into the living room and threw more logs on the fire and a couple of pillows in place for him to lean on. "You'll be more yourself soon."

After handing her his wet clothing, he turned to the pillows on the floor in front of the fire. Evidently he had problems following her instructions to take a seat with his robe wrapped tightly enough to make it hard for him to bend.

Her eyes widened as he'd lean one way, yank at a corner of the robe, then stand fully upright again, only to repeat his motions.

"This isn't a side show, Stell," he groused as he finally managed to kneel.

She tossed her head, then indicated the bundle of sopping clothing in her arms. "I'll go put these in the dryer, then put on some coffee. Make yourself at home."

Quin didn't budge until she'd left the room;

then he hunkered down on the pillows. He hadn't realized he was so modest until he'd noticed her watching.

Relaxing and allowing the warmth from the burning logs to soothe him, he inhaled deeply. The aroma of freshly baked apple pies, mixed with pungent wood smoke, almost blocked out the fusty scent of his wet hair.

Stella's home felt comfortable in every sense of the word. The furniture was just worn enough, without looking threadbare, that he wouldn't have to worry about staining it. The furnishings were designed with comfort in mind, with only a few knick-knacks lying around and nothing too fru-fru.

The coffee table behind his back was made of heavy, dark wood and a few magazines had been scattered on its surface. The sofa behind it was covered in a heavy plaid fabric. Over the mantle, Stella had mounted a Monet print depicting flowers. The room contained nothing overly feminine, but just enough touches of lace to give a gentle and soothing feel. Romantic, like her.

He heard the sound of the clothes dryer in the background, then the aroma of coffee blended with the other scents. Within minutes, Stella came into the room, bearing a tray with two mugs and a platter of cheese and crackers. She slid the tray onto the coffee table.

"Why did you play hide and seek with Ian after

I told you not to?" she asked, looking at him as if he were an alien.

Possibly he was to her, at least alien in the sense of strange and unknown. Although they'd been incredibly close as kids, they'd both gone through a lot of growing up. Although he doubted the Troublemakers' rumor that Stella was the sensationalist author, he didn't know her as well as he'd once thought he did. And yet, there she stood with a strand of hair in her eyes, looking eerily like the kid she once was. Yet there was nothing childlike about her.

It was confusing.

She was confusing.

She'd gotten him so confused, he no longer knew what he was doing—except he knew he enjoyed her company. Sitting with her in front of the fire was even better than he'd wished for when he'd been stuck in the basement. "I told Ian I wouldn't play, but he dashed into the basement anyway. I had no choice but to follow him."

"You could have left him down there." She took a seat on the sofa, as if putting as much distance between them as possible while maintaining an air of friendliness.

"In retrospect, I wish I had." Quin patted a pillow beside him. "I want to look at both you *and* the fire. Come sit by me."

Stella gulped nervously, but did as he requested.

Something about the way she was too careful not to touch him, even accidently, told him she was as aware of him as he was of her. He could feel each breath she drew in almost as if her breath were his. A fragile pulse beat rapidly on the side of her neck nearest him. An urge to kiss that pulse became stronger and stronger.

Stella must have seen something in his face, however, because she quickly rose and mumbled something about checking on her pies. Quin took a couple of gulps of coffee, restoring the feeling in his fingers which had become numb from the cold. The returning sensations were almost painfully intense.

When Stella didn't return right away, he became restless. Deciding to find out what was keeping her so long, he got up and went into the kitchen. The room was empty, but he heard her in the laundry room. As he approached the doorway into the laundry room, he saw that her head was in the dryer. He could only hope she was checking on the clothes and not planning to climb in.

He could get into this whole domestic routine if it meant he had Stella to keep him entertained. "Need some help?"

Chapter Nine

"Ouch." Stella bumped her head as she pulled it out of the dryer. Why'd he have to come sneaking up on her? "No. It'll be awhile, yet."

Quin took a step closer and filled up all the breathing space in her suddenly too small laundry room. It had always seemed big enough before. But now with him lurking so near, she could lean her head forward and brush her face against his chest, she realized the room was far too small.

Maybe she should have it enlarged, she thought, seizing onto any thought that would keep her mind off Quin and how it would feel to have his arms around her again.

"Are you hurt? Let me check your head," he

said before doing what she'd really hoped he wouldn't do. He touched her.

It was a gentle probing with his fingertips against her tender scalp, yet she felt it burn all the way to her toes. Not because she was in pain, but because it was Quin who touched her.

He lifted her and she could tell by the stern expression on his face that his ribs must still be very sore. She'd weighed in that morning and the scale had registered one hundred twenty-eight pounds, so she knew she was no light weight, yet he didn't struggle at all. He placed her atop the washing machine, then parted her hair to take a look at where she'd bumped her head.

"It's fine, really." Pulling back, she tried to shrug away from him, but he didn't back away. He came nearer instead, cupping her chin in his palm.

"Stella," he whispered. "I'd like to kiss you again, but I don't want to if it's something you don't want."

The wisest course of action, she knew, would be to say a simple "no." It was what he expected her to say. But how could she say no with his dark eyes looking so intently into hers? When she could feel the heat of his fingers on her face?

It would be dumb to say yes. But what harm could one little kiss do?

Besides, her vocal chords were frozen, as was

her ability to ever tell him no, regardless of how often she told him she would. Or how often she told herself she could. It was only a tiny word, after all.

She must have done something right because within seconds his lips covered hers. His kiss was like hot chocolate on an icy day. A rush of warmth traveled down her throat, into her stomach, and then out all her nerve endings.

It was really strange to think her childhood best friend could do such delicious things to her senses.

Her fingers closed over the leather strap he wore around his neck, only to reveal an acorn. A warm, mushy feeling nudged its way into her midsection. After all these years, he wore the acorn she'd made for him.

Who would ever have thought it?

He hadn't forgotten her or the promises they'd made to each other as children. They'd both done a lot of growing up, but his wearing the acorn necklace proved there was still much of the boy she'd worshiped dwelling within the man in her arms.

A ray of sunshine traveled through her heart—then a warning seemed to sound inside her.

She almost pulled away, then realized that whether Quin remained in town or not, whether he'd make her fall in love with him and then disappear for another ten years or for life, she couldn't live with herself if she didn't have his kisses tonight to remember for always.

She hadn't wanted to admit, even to herself, that she'd always been in love with him. Some part of her must have hoped that one day Quin would come home to her. It had made breaking up with Dexter so very easy. She'd been settling then for second best and deep inside, she'd known it.

She'd waited for some other man to make her feel what Quin drew out in her automatically. It had never happened.

It was right that his, and only his, kiss could make her forget that her heart would be broken come morning, because her heart fluttered for Quin and only Quin.

What was it about Stella that was unforgettable, Quin wondered? A man could lose himself in a woman like her. Desire to grant her wishes and hopes and dreams could make him forget his own goals and desires.

He was supposed to be careful and remember there were rapids ahead. The only problem was that he liked rapids and they had nothing over Stella.

He didn't want to be careful when it came to Stella. All he wanted was to win one of her smiles, earn one of her giggles, and steal another kiss.

Man, he had it bad.

Chapter Ten

Quin gazed into her eyes and somehow, it made her feel shy. As she responded by ducking her head, she heard another noise, something remarkably like the sound of tin foil hitting linoleum. Tin foil?

Stella froze in place, listening for more, and Quin turned his head toward the kitchen as well. All at once it hit her. Tramp. "My pies!"

With a speed that might have qualified her for the Olympics, Stella threw herself off the washing machine and dashed into the kitchen. Quin followed.

There, on the floor in front of her, lay three empty pie pans, and the contents of the fourth was quickly gobbled up by an extremely happy, and extremely replete, hellhound.

"Bad dog," said Stella as she made shooing motions at the animal. She felt sick inside.

Quin didn't say anything. He merely headed back into the laundry room. She heard the sound of the dryer opening and knew he was getting dressed.

She didn't know whether to whimper, sob, or feel relieved. Spending time with Quin was dangerous to her peace of mind, but what she hadn't realized was he could make her forget common sense.

Perhaps Tramp had done the best thing in his hunger, or possibly jealousy, since he always seemed to act up when she and Quin were too busy with each other to pay attention to him. Unfortunately, his consumption of her pies meant a whole lot of work for her, since they were due at the fair in the morning.

The clock above the range showed it was after midnight already, and now she had at least a couple of hours of work ahead of her to remake the destroyed pies. Fortunately, she had enough premade dough in the freezer, but this would mean thawing it in warm water. She'd have to slice more apples since she'd used up the ones she'd already cut when making the first dozen pies.

Quin came back into the kitchen, fully dressed,

with his shirt sleeves rolled up and ready for action. Clapping his hands together, he said, "I've got a great idea. How's about we bake us some pies?"

"Good plan. How are you at slicing apples?"

Feigning a French accent, and a really bad one at that, he said, "Et eez moi speciality. Am not I zee famous Chef Gregorie?"

Stella tossed him an apple. "Get busy."

She was really lucky that if she had to fall head over heels for a guy, it was a wonderful man like Quin. What a good sport he was. He seemed to know how upset she was without her having to say a word. Even as kids, he'd been able to sense her inner turmoil.

As he deftly cored, then sliced an apple, his gaze met hers and she felt as if a zillion Christmas bulbs lit up inside her. Why did he have to be an adventurer? Why couldn't he want what she did, a place to settle down and raise a family and to discover what life and love could offer?

She wouldn't think of that now, she told herself, placing the frozen dough in the warm water she'd run in the sink.

After he left there would be plenty of time for regrets. While he remained in Littlemouth, she'd focus on the here and now and not what was to come. It was the only way to enjoy what little time she had with him. Who knew when, if ever, he'd come home to her again?

By the time Stella slipped the four new pies into the oven and set the timer, the clock read one-thirty. The remaining pies were placed far back on the counter out of Tramp's reach. Quin stood at the sink, washing his hands. The kitchen was filled with the aroma of apples and cinnamon and Stella's frazzled nerves.

She kept shooting nervous glimpses at him out of the corner of her eye and he was curious what she'd finally say or do. He could let her off the stick by going home, but he was hoping she'd fess up to whatever was eating at her.

A smile hovered at the corner of his mouth, but he couldn't seem to wipe it away. She was so adorable standing by the stove, alternately wiping her hands on her clothing or rubbing at an imaginary spot on the counter with a crumpled paper towel. And the looks she kept shooting him, curiosity mixed with embarrassment.

Then she cocked her head at him and said with a trembling voice, "Quin? If you don't kiss me again, I don't know what I'll do. I think maybe explode."

He couldn't bear to disappoint her. "Can you hold off long enough to sit in front of the fire?"

She nodded.

After closing the kitchen door so Tramp couldn't escape, he led Stella into the living room, helping her take a seat on the floor in front of the hearth. He tossed another log on the fire, fighting a nagging doubt about whether he should leave.

As they snuggled in front of the fire, he brushed his lips against hers. He'd kissed a lot of women in his checkered past, but a kiss had never before felt quite so fulfilling.

Stella was excitement, amusement, and everything good all rolled into one bundle of delicious woman. Tucking her head beneath his chin, the tension in his body relaxed for the first time in many months.

The moon shone brightly in the predawn hours, lighting up the dew on Stella's shrubbery. A figure dressed all in black sidled through the shrubbery, then peered through a window. A lizard on a nearby bush, frightened by the movement, quickly darted away.

Four more figures in black noiselessly joined the first at the window.

"So sweet. Sleeping like children on the floor." Miss Tipplemouse sighed, obviously overcome by sentiment.

"See? I told you Quin was here," added Cait triumphantly.

Debby looked concerned. "The fire's gone out. Do you think Quin is warm enough?"

Janice laughed, but didn't say anything. There was no need.

"It appears our plan is working." Prissy Goody nodded, pleased with their efforts. "Your rescue idea certainly appears to have done the trick, Cait."

"All it took was a dear little five-year-old."

They all laughed because Ian, while dear, generally was not described so fondly.

The women crept from the window as soundlessly as they'd arrived, then walked to the front of the house.

There, they were met—with a glaring flashlight in their faces. Deputy Sheriff Brendan McCade said, "Hold it right there."

"Is that you, Brendan?" asked Cait.

"Yes, Ma'am." By that point, he recognized the Troublemakers and only curiosity kept him shining the light at them. "How are you, this morning?"

"Fine, Sheriff. Just fine."

"Mind if I ask what you were up to?"

"Just taking an early morning stroll," replied Prissy.

"Through Stella's shrubbery?"

"I'll say," piped up Miss Tipplemouse.

Brendan's lips trembled as he fought to keep from laughing. The women were always up to something—usually no good, but nothing actually illegal. He was sure if he asked Stella about it, she'd tell him that her mother and friends always trampled through her yard every predawn.

Although he was tempted to take them in "for questioning," just to tease them a little, he thought better of it because the fair was due to open in only a few hours. He'd be in hot water if it didn't open as scheduled. Being wise in the ways of Littlemouth, he signaled that they could go. "It's dark out, so you ladies need to be careful."

Janice switched on a flashlight and said with a husky drawl, "Oh, Sheriff, we're *always* careful."

Quin had never considered himself in the least bit artistic, other than how he managed to create a journalistic style with his words, but looking at Stella as she slept made him feel positively poetic. He wasn't sure how it had happened, but they'd both fallen asleep on the floor in front of the fire.

It was cozy and rather than fleeing, he was occupied composing a poem. If only he could find a good word to rhyme with dawn.

Lawn.

Mowing.

Settling down. The thought yanked him out of his romantic fog.

The fire had long since died and he couldn't remember having slept this well in years.

Heck, most of the time, he only half slept for fear a vicious drug lord or dictator would send someone to silence his pen. Although his life wasn't now at stake, certainly his lifestyle was. So why did he feel so peaceful?

One glance at Stella told him everything he needed to know. They'd belonged to each other for as long as he could remember. The knowledge gave him strength when he'd been thrown in jail in Moscow, the time he'd been lost in a Brazilian jungle, and when those bandits tossed him out of the car. He could pretend otherwise, tell himself he only wanted to get to know her better, but the truth was, he wanted to be with her forever.

However, things weren't so easy. He had a job to return to, a job he found fulfilling and intriguing. Sure it was lonely, but was he ready to toss it all in to play house in Littlemouth, inspiring though the idea might be?

The last thing he wanted to do was hurt Stella, but wasn't that what they were heading toward? He wanted to protect her, even if it meant protecting her from himself.

Bottom line, he was selfish and didn't deserve a woman like Stella.

He rose quietly, not wanting to disturb her because they'd both been up late making the pies that were due at the fairgrounds soon.

Only a jerk would leave without saying something, but how could he say anything until he fig-ured it out for himself? He didn't want to consider what would happen if his mother or one of her pals learned where he'd been all night. Leaving immediately would, he hoped, keep Stella's rep-utation intact.

He made a beeline to the kitchen.

Tramp barked a happy greeting when Quin opened the door into the kitchen, but he quickly hushed him. The more he thought about it, the more it seemed that giving Stella, and himself, time to think things through was a good idea.

He opened the outer door into the yard so Tramp could go out. Taking a seat on the back steps, he watched as the dog energetically circled the yard a time or two before getting down to the serious business of sniffing around the oak tree.

Quin wiped the sleep from his eyes, literally as well as figuratively. How much had Stella changed? Would she expect him to remain in Lit-tlemouth or was it possible she'd like to come with him? Did he want to expose her to that kind of danger? How much could *he* change? Could he become the kind of guy she deserved?

Calling Tramp back inside, Quin put all the pies into the large box Stella had set aside for taking them to the fair. They were heavier than he'd ex-pected them to be, but if he walked home with them, he could get a shower and then drive the rest of the way.

As quietly as possible, he entered the living room. Stella's cherrywood hair had billowed out around her, making her look as though she slept on a cloud. She was so beautiful, intelligent—and precious.

His chest became tight. She felt so right in his arms.

Before his resolve to leave crumbled, he rushed back to the kitchen and safety. He then tiptoed out her back door with the box of pies in his arms instead of the woman he wanted there.

Chapter Eleven

When Quin neared his house, he hoped to sneak in without anyone the wiser. No need to create more gossip for Stella to live down. He opened his rental car door and carefully placed the box of pies on the back seat.

He climbed the steps to his house, then slid the house key his mom had given him into the lock. Strange, it didn't meet any resistance. Pushing the door open, his gaze met a gaggle of gossips.

TROUBLE, every last one of 'em, were sitting in the front room with expressions much like Tramp's after he'd gotten into Stella's pies.

Quin gulped. So much for coming in secretly. They had probably gathered to make an early start for the fairgrounds. Interestingly, they were all dressed head to toe in identical black shirts and slacks. "Good morning, ladies. Why all the black? Are you going to a funeral?"

"We're dressed in costumes for the fair. How are you this morning?"

"Just fine." If he didn't know them better, he'd think they'd been out skulking around in the dark, peeping in windows and hunting for gossip.

"Good morning, Quinlan," said his mother with a wry smile on her face. "About time you showed up."

"I couldn't sleep so I brought Stella's pies for the fair." It was close enough to the truth, and might protect her from wagging tongues.

"Where are they then?" asked Prissy.

"In my car."

"Then why are you here instead of the fairgrounds?" asked Cait calmly, making his answers resemble Swiss cheese.

"I wanted to change clothes first?" Even as he replied, he knew how weak an excuse it was, and how one look at his face made clear that he hadn't shaved since the previous day. His clothing was the worse for wear—and water balloons—as well.

Prissy confirmed his fears by adding, in a worried tone, "I see. You didn't bother cleaning up before visiting my daughter?"

"The scraggly look is in vogue." Not waiting to

hear them argue the point, he exited the room, then headed into the hall bath and out of earshot.

Meanwhile in the living room, Debby passed around a dish of pastries and each woman took one. "When Ian's mother called, I was a little surprised that Quin had offered to babysit. Water balloons. How humiliating for my son."

Janice couldn't keep from laughing. "Ian surpassed himself this time."

"I enjoyed watching Quin squirm, but I'm a little disappointed that Stella did the rescuing instead of vice versa," replied Prissy. "Although, it's possible that if she'd been the one to watch Ian, there might not have been a need for rescue. She's always been good with children."

"It probably doesn't matter who saved whom," added Debby.

Cait said, between bites, "I believe this is the second time Stella rescued him. First the dumpster and now the basement."

"I almost laughed out loud when Quin mentioned the scraggly look being in vogue," Janice said.

Cait nodded. "And the expression on his face was priceless when he first walked in and saw us waiting for him."

"His ego was getting a little too healthy," said

Janice. "A little role reversal won't do him any harm."

They all nodded, then put their heads together to discuss their further plans. As they concluded, Prissy's brow was furrowed in thought. "Do you think I could hint to Ian that Millicent loves water balloons?"

Less than an hour later, Quin arrived at the fair-grounds. As he meandered around looking for the Trouble Tarts booth, he was still surprised that when he'd emerged from the bathroom earlier none of the Troublemakers had remained behind to question him further. Usually they were worse than hounds baying at a fox when it came to gossip.

Maybe his story had held up better than he'd thought?

At last, he discovered the Trouble Tarts booth just past a tent with a huge sign of a crystal ball and the word *psychic* written in squiggly print. Discretely, beneath the sign was a placard stating: "$3.00/reading, all proceeds benefit the Little-mouth Sheriff's Department Benevolence Fund."

Seemed like a good cause, he thought, making a mental note to have his fortune told later. Some-how, he suspected it might involve travel, falling in love with a dark-headed stranger, and coming into a small sum of money.

His mother manned the Trouble Tarts booth, busily slicing pies and putting each piece on a paper plate. She looked up when she heard him put the cardboard box on the table she'd set up behind her. "There you are."

Quin nodded, shoving his hands into his jeans pockets.

She handed him a long apron saying, "Put this on to protect your clothing. You'd be surprised how messy handling pies can be."

"I'm just the delivery man. I'm not handling any pies."

"Don't stand there and argue. We're counting on you to help increase our revenues. Everyone in town will want to meet Littlemouth's most famous citizen, and they'll have to buy a slice of pie to get at you. Irma has big plans for the money this booth is going to raise."

Quin knew better than to argue with his mother. If he didn't readily agree to her demands, she'd find some way to blackmail him into it. He didn't have the energy to defend himself today, not after his encounter with Ian the night before. "How long will I have to do this?"

"We're booked to work at the Ladies Auxiliary sale for the next few hours."

"Hours? How long is this going to take?" Quin grabbed his side and rubbed his ribs, all the while trying to keep a smile off his face and to look pitiful.

"Stella should be here before too long. She can help you. Besides, you'll probably sell out of pies before lunchtime. There's only six dozen of them."

She must have caught on that he was brimming with good health. Otherwise, she'd have him back in bed and be feeding him more chicken soup before he could have finished a sentence.

Six dozen pies meant seventy-two pies. At six slices per pie . . .

Three hundred, four hundred? More? Quin's mental multiplication failed him. He grimaced, figuring that however many slices that equaled, it was more pie than he wanted to deal with. Somehow, his mother's estimate of his pie-selling abilities seemed optimistic, even for her. Narrowing his eyes, he wondered what exactly she was up to.

She blew him a kiss and darted away, before he had a chance to stop her.

By ten o'clock, he'd managed to sell three dozen pies by telling everyone he'd personally made the pie. Of course, he'd long since lost track of which were the four pies he'd sliced apples for, but it was for a good cause, the Littlemouth Library, and each slice sold would get him out of the booth faster. Thankfully, a number of people had bought entire pies, or he'd be at this all week.

He shuddered as The Gargoyle approached his

booth with a sour-grapes expression pursing her lips. As far as he was concerned, however, that seemed to be her natural expression. "Enjoying the fair, Mrs. Gordon?"

"Enjoying it as much as I could expect to." She stood on the opposite side of the table, ogling his pies. "I heard you made these pies personally?"

Quin shrugged. "Some of them."

Pointing to the pie he was serving slices from, she asked, "Did you make that one?"

Expecting a quick sale, he grinned proudly. "Sure did."

"How about the one next to it?"

"That one, too."

"How about those two in the corner?"

Quin turned to see which pies she meant before it hit him why she was asking which of the pies were the ones *he'd* made. "No, I definitely had no hand in making those two beautiful pies."

He hoped he told the truth, but as far as he was concerned, one pie looked very much like the next. He had no way of knowing any longer which of the pies had come from Stella's.

"Good," said The Gargoyle gloatingly. "I'll take both of the pies you *didn't* make."

Once Mrs. Gordon had made her way from the booth, there was a momentary lull in business. Quin leaned against the back of the table in order to take some weight off his feet, which were throbbing from standing on them so long.

Since there wasn't a chair in the booth, he was tempted to take a seat on the hard ground. Just as he began sinking, a red-headed urchin approached.

"Are you playing hide and seek?" Ian asked excitedly.

"No. I'm not hiding," Quin quickly jumped to his feet.

"What were you doing under the table, then?"

"I wasn't under it. I was stooping."

"Why were you stooping?"

The kid simply wasn't going to let this drop. "I was, um, checking my supply of water balloons."

"Cool." Ian grinned, revealing a gap from a missing front tooth. How could such a bratty kid look so cute and innocent?

"Are you here for pie?"

"What kinda pie?"

"Apple. Want some?"

Ian fumbled in his pocket. "I gots thirty-nine cents."

"Sold." Quin pulled some change from his own pocket and added it to the kitty.

As he gave the pie to the boy, he heard a young voice call, "Innnn."

"Mary Alice." Ian covered his face with his hands as a blond-haired pixie hurried toward them.

"I told her my name's not *In*, but she just won't listen."

"Girl troubles, I see," said Quin.

Ian took one last frightened look over his shoulder, then hightailed it out of there, leaving Quin stuck with the pie.

Mary Alice arrived at the booth, looking forlorn. "Where'd he go?"

"I think he went to find his mother," Quin told her. A wicked thought occurred to him. He knew exactly how he could get even with Ian. "I think he likes you because he bought this piece of pie for you."

The girl grinned in delight. "Thank you."

She accepted the pie, then dashed off in the same direction as Ian had gone.

Despite its small size, or maybe because of it, Littlemouth was a friendly town. Old acquaintances, good friends, young and old, all came to the booth to say howdy, clap him on the back, or shake his hand. They had a way of making even a wanderer like Quin feel he'd finally returned home. Some part of him would always belong to this town and consider it home, no matter where life and adventure led him.

It wasn't a bad little place at all.

His heart rate suddenly sped up. Scanning the crowd milling around the fairgrounds, he searched for Stella because he knew his heart wouldn't react like that unless she was somewhere around, watching him. Then their gazes locked. She was still some distance away, but she stared right at him.

Boy, was she a sight for tired eyes. She had to be the most beautiful woman he'd ever laid eyes on. She was a natural beauty, not the kind of beauty based on symmetry of facial features, but the sort that glowed from an inner sweetness.

Shooting him a bright grin as she approached the booth, she slipped under the table and joined him. "I feared you'd absconded with my pies."

"I thought you needed your beauty sleep." He considered greeting her with a kiss, but she didn't make any sign she expected it. "I can see the sleep worked. You look great."

"Thanks. But don't think I'm buying your line of compliments. You snuck out because you were afraid to face me. Admit it," she said with a joking voice that had him wondering if she meant it or not. Was she aware of how right she was about him? As she'd been correct all along, he told himself, wondering how she always seemed to know him better than he knew himself.

"I was afraid you were embarrassed after last night—you know." She ducked her head so he couldn't see her eyes.

Quin forgot about the crowds, forgot they weren't alone, and dragged her into his arms. "That's the last thing I'd want you to think. Being with you is incredible, so good it scares me. I was confused."

He gently pulled her chin so she faced him.

"Are you confused now?" she asked.

"Yes, but not about one thing. I love spending time with you."

"What are you confused about?"

"Whether or not I can bear leaving you."

"Oh." Stella didn't say anything else, but she dropped her arms and stepped out of his embrace.

"Don't be mad?"

"I'm not mad," she whispered.

Just then, a customer approached the booth and requested two pieces of pie. As Quin deftly cut the slices, Stella leaned toward him.

Her nearness did strange and wonderful things to his heart. Then she said, "If you sell out of pies, I'll let you go slug hunting with me again. This time *you* can do the salt."

Chapter Twelve

All it took was a hint of a reward and it was amazing how quickly Quin managed to sell out of pie, including buying the last six full pies himself.

"Nothing like giving a guy an incentive," said Stella. Hopeful. She felt completely, pie in the sky, Mary Poppins hopeful. Maybe Quin wouldn't leave after all?

Right. That was about as likely as the kids at school begging for more homework. But Quin's not wanting to leave her was at least something upon which to build. "I'll make us some sandwiches, if you're hungry?"

"Believe me, when you're around, I always work up an appetite. I need to find my mom, though, and give her the money from the booth."

"Why don't you go look for her, then meet me at home? I'll take your pies with me and you can pick them up there."

"How about a kiss first, to whet my appetite?"

"I suspect it's whetted enough," she replied, as she leaned forward to kiss him anyway. She'd been wanting to do it all morning but hadn't known how he'd react.

She especially didn't want to appear to be possessive. Public kissing would show the whole town she'd placed her brand on him. But if he was amenable, she was more than willing to haul out the ol' branding iron.

When he took her in his arms, she placed her hand on his chest, feeling the staccato beat of his heart. Their lips came together with far more sweetness than she'd expected.

Now that she'd thrown caution to the wind, she might as well enjoy being a total fool. There was no turning back now.

She loved Quin, wholeheartedly, completely. Not being with him while he was in Littlemouth would hurt her, in the long run, far more than if she wrung out every moment of his attention at her disposal. Once he was gone, she'd have plenty of time to deal with her broken heart.

In the meantime, they had magic.

* * *

"*Psst*. He's coming," whispered Janice Smith, who'd been elected TROUBLE lookout for the duration of the fair. "Places everyone."

"It took him long enough," complained Cait. Debby sent her a censuring glare and she silenced her complaints. Each of the ladies quickly took their seats circling the satin-draped table in the center of the pyschic's tent.

At the sound of Quin's approaching footsteps, Janice leaned toward Prissy and said, "Believe me, I heard it on the *best* authority."

Prissy feigned a look of surprise, deliberately overacting for all she was worth. "My daughter would never do top-secret experiments—not even for the government."

"Well," opined Cait. "I daresay you wouldn't be allowed to divulge a word if it were true. Plus, her job at the high school would make a good cover, if one *cared* to do secret experiments."

"I'll say," said Irma. Then, as she'd carefully been coached, she added, her voice only wavering a bit since a man could overhear her, "Have you been in her toolshed? All those shelves full of *hazardous* chemicals."

"Who would need such things for gardenin—" Cait cut off her words and gave a dramatic shake of her head. "Why, Quinlan, we expected to see you much sooner."

"I thought I was fast," he said. "What are you talking about?"

"We were just discussing the likelihood of there being a spy in our midst," said Janice.

"Yes, we've heard there are some experiments taking place in Littlemouth," added Cait. "You don't know anything about it, do you?"

Janice piped in, "Maybe you're home in order to track down a spy?"

"I'd love a hot story, but I'm here on vacation, not to track down agents. What does it have to do with Stella, anyway?"

"Absolutely nothing," Prissy answered quickly—perhaps too quickly. They all seemed to clam up at once.

He searched their faces but they were pros at schooling their expressions. "If you hear anything else, let me know."

"Oh, we don't have any facts," Janice said.

"Just supposition," said Cait. "No use telling a reporter anything but facts . . . But Stella *is* a rather interesting young woman, don't you think?"

"She's fascinating." Quin came further into the tent, feeling as if he'd had a gallon of water poured over his head. They'd been gossiping about his Stella. The woman of his dreams. The one who was a high school teacher, loved to sew, and helped build tree houses. Now he was supposed to believe she was some secret government scientist?

No way. Although—it might explain why she'd been so upset when Tramp dug up her seedlings. He didn't know what to believe.

"We sold all the pies." Handing the strongbox to his mother, he tore off his apron and wadded it into a ball. "I need to head out now."

"Where are you off to in such a hurry?" asked his mother.

"Stella asked me to help her out, eh, with some slugs."

His mother arched one brow and he had a feeling his excuses were sounding weaker and weaker.

"She also promised to make me a sandwich."

They gave him a knowing look.

His mother shooed him away. "Run along, dear. We appreciate your help with the booth."

Quin didn't have quite the urgency to get to Stella's place he'd had only moments earlier, before hearing the latest gossip about her. He'd think it was outrageous gossip if Stella's own mother hadn't been part of the discussion. Maybe he should place a few discrete calls to one of the Washington correspondents? They might know what project she could be working on. However, if it was top secret, that might blow her cover entirely, and he wasn't willing to do that.

Stella appeared to be happy in Littlemouth. She'd grown up here and it seemed clear it's where she planned to live out her life. If whatever she might be doing for the government was important, would she have to stop if it became common knowledge? Or worse yet, would she be forced to relocate?

No matter how much his reporter's nose twitched to find out the facts, he couldn't do that to her. He dismissed the dark thought that rose in his mind that if she was forced to leave Littlemouth, perhaps she could join him in his travels.

Besides, the women were probably mistaken. Yet—there was one sure way to find out. Truth could be uncovered in other ways. He'd need only the most elementary of his skills: stealth and hands-on snooping. He'd scope out her toolshed.

Stella made short work of preparing lunch for Quin. She covered the table in a cheerful red and white checkered tablecloth and set an especially lush African violet plant in the center.

Just as she laid cloth napkins on the table, she heard a loud noise outside. Dashing to the back door, she looked out but didn't see anything. Tramp was being good for once and resting beneath the kitchen table, although his ears were alert and his excuse for a tail wagged like a metronome.

Just then, she heard another crash, sending a bolt of fear down her spine. Grabbing the portable phone and the baseball bat she kept beside the backdoor, she called Tramp.

The dog ran past her in a streak, down the stairs and directly to the toolshed. But rather than growling as Stella expected from what she'd hoped would be a fine watchdog, Tramp jumped on the shed door with his front two paws, yipping happily.

"Quin?" It had to be him. "Is that you?"

Hearing no reply, she approached the shed and pounded on the door with the tip of her bat. "I've got a phone and I'm calling 911 now. If it's not you, Quin, then whoever it is had better stay inside because I'm armed."

"It's me, Stell," came the reply. At last, the shed door opened a crack to reveal the idiot wearing a sheepish grin. With a sense of impatience, she remembered the bathrobe incident of the day before, and wondered how often she'd have to speak to him through partially opened doors.

"What are you doing in there? And what was that racket?"

Quin swung the door open the rest of the way and bent to give Tramp a reassuring pat. "Um, well, I was curious. I've always wanted to look in your shed."

"For heaven's sake, Quin. Why?"

"I'm a reporter." He shrugged. "I love to snoop?"

That wasn't a very good explanation and he knew it because he had a guilty expression on his face.

"Did you break anything?" she asked, trying to peek past him to survey the damage.

"I don't think so." Quin stepped back and pointed toward the back corner of the shed. "I was stooping down and my hip knocked against that shelf. It toppled."

Stella glanced in the direction he indicated. Cans of potting soil and some of her gardening implements lay on the ground along with the shelf he'd butted against. "I've got only one question. Why were you stooping down?"

Quin rubbed the toe of his shoe against the rough wooden floor. "To read the bottles."

Had he lost his mind? Maybe all those years out in a cold dark world had taken a toll on his sanity? "Why would you want to read them?"

"I was curious about what chemicals you were using on your garden." He didn't look her in the eye.

"You couldn't just ask me? Besides, I recycle the bottles from the high school. The labels don't mean anything."

"Oh. Well."

"You're not making any sense. Are you sure you're okay?" He didn't seem ill—just extremely guilty about something. "Why don't you come in and eat the lunch I made?"

He allowed her to lead him into the house and took a seat at the table. Despite her job as a biology teacher, she didn't know much about controlled substances. Surely he didn't think she kept anything that could be distilled to make a dangerous chemical? Surely he hadn't developed an addiction?

Placing her hand over his, she said, "You trust me, don't you?"

"That's exactly the question I was about ask you," he said. "If you had a secret, you'd tell me, wouldn't you? We always shared our secrets."

"Well, if I had a secret and it created a problem for me, then I certainly would. I'm here for you if you have a problem. You know I'd understand?"

"I have a problem?" he asked as his brows drew together.

"It's not surprising, really, when you think about it. I mean, all alone in those foreign countries." Stella shrugged, "Who could blame you if you wanted to escape?"

Quin said nothing.

"We could go into Wichita to get you help." She took a seat beside him, bringing a hand up to cup his face. "No one in Littlemouth would have to find out. Unlike our mothers, Quin, I don't gossip."

"You think I need help?" Quin pulled her hand down. "Just what are you accusing me of?"

"I'm not accusing you of anything. I just wanted to assure you that if you had a problem, I'd see you through it."

"Stella!"

"Yes?"

"I don't have that kind of problem."

"You don't?"

"The only kind of problem I have is in following your chain of logic."

"You have a logic problem? Join the club! What on earth were you doing in my shed?"

"Investigating."

"Oookay." Stella puffed with frustration at her bangs. "Care to explain?"

"I suppose I do owe you an explanation," he said, sounding as if he were completely rational which of course he couldn't be. She couldn't think of any sane explanation for his actions.

"Start with the truth?" she suggested mildly.

"I heard a rumor about you and I wanted to find out for myself if it was true or not."

"And what did this rumor have to do with my toolshed?" Stella placed a hand over her mouth. "No. Don't tell me. You thought I was making dangerous chemicals."

"No. That's not it."

"Well, I'd like to know what it is."

"I heard you were doing top-secret scientific experimentation for the government."

Stella couldn't hold back a shocked laugh. "You honestly believed I'd be qualified to do any such thing? That the government just farms out top secret experiments to any ol' high school teacher for the asking?"

"I hadn't thought about it that way, Stell. Honestly, though, you're special. You're bright and clever and more than capable of doing it. You're like a superwoman."

"Why I think that's the nicest compliment you've ever paid me, Quin, even if it is patently delusional."

Quin slumped his forehead onto hers. "Thank heavens. I was losing my mind."

"Why couldn't you have asked me?"

"I was afraid you wouldn't be allowed to reveal it if it was true. So I figured I'd better find out for myself and look for evidence. I have to admit, those chemical bottles gave me quite a shock."

"You're a sorry case, Quinlan Gregory."

"I know."

"Promise me one thing." Again she cupped his face in her palm. "In the future, if you have any questions about me, just ask. I promise to be as truthful as I know how."

Now that he knew she wasn't a superwoman or a spy, Quin breathed a huge sigh of relief. He loved Stella as he'd always thought of her. Sweet and uncomplicated, gardening, sewing, and teaching kids science.

Adding bestselling novelist to the list had been hard for him to accept, but the idea that she was a secret agent had nearly driven him berserk because it placed her so far out of his reach.

When he'd first seen her again, he felt a bit smugly superior with all his worldly experience. He'd been a dumb guy—he admitted it.

However, he'd always imagined Stella waiting for him to come home. Everything he'd learned about her since returning proved that assumption false.

He considered the possibility Stella might not want him. It wasn't simply a case of making up his own mind, but rather, of making her see him as her equal, as someone she could fall in love with.

Earlier, when he'd heard the Troublemakers gossiping, he could feel Stella evaporating from his grasp. As if she were so far above his league, he hadn't a hope of ever capturing her heart.

The thought of losing her made him admit just what she meant to him. Wherever Stella was, he'd find both excitement and home.

Why hadn't he realized it before? Sure, he'd been determined to travel, to find life and adventure, but why had he been blind to the fact it was here with her?

Somehow, he must have known it all along. Why else had he brought Tramp to her? Why else would he head to her whenever he was confused? Travel and excitement lost their luster when there was no home to return to.

Stella was his home. Additionally, she was the most exciting woman he'd ever met or would likely ever meet. Fortunately for him, he had her where he wanted her.

Seated beside him.

Within his reach.

Chapter Thirteen

Stella saw embers flare to life in the depth of Quin's eyes. He whispered, "I love you, Stell."

"Do you mean it?"

"Uh-hmm," he answered, lightly brushing his finger tip against her lips. "There's something I want to ask you."

Hope fluttered like butterfly wings in her stomach. "Yes?"

"I'm going to have to leave Littlemouth soon. Come with me?"

At least he'd learned something. He'd learned to ask. Nonetheless, she was disappointed. She'd hoped he'd stay right here at home in Littlemouth with her. Did she love him enough to leave? To give up everything and everyone she loved?

Yes. She could answer with a clear conscience. There was no doubt in her mind.

That wasn't the problem.

The problem was he didn't love her enough to do the same. She wasn't sure she could cope with the idea that she loved him more. Love wasn't supposed to be a contest with a winner and a loser, but a sharing, each offering the same love and trust to the other.

When she didn't answer right away, he leaned back, then stood. "I guess that's all I need to know."

She ought to be thrilled he asked her. Instead, her heart was already broken and he hadn't left her yet. Her lack of response was a final blow, but she couldn't get words to form.

He turned and left the room and she heard the silence of the door closing.

She should never have hoped. Quin would always be a wanderer and she was forever doomed to be a homebody.

Quin felt stiff all over. He'd been sitting in the tree house for over two hours, certain Stella was in her house, and hoping she'd come talk with him. Surely he could find something to say that would make things right between them.

Her silence had given him an answer—the wrong answer. Stella was the kind of woman who wouldn't be satisfied with anything less than marriage, and for her that meant putting down roots in Littlemouth. She'd never be satisfied with anything less.

He pulled a well-thumbed volume of *Pride and Prejudice* from the chair beside him and opened it. Maybe it would keep him occupied. However, it didn't, just as it hadn't the last six times he'd opened it.

"Yo," called a masculine voice which Quin thought he recognized. Glimpsing out the window, he saw Brendan dressed in the sheriff's uniform which seemed so incongruous on a guy he'd once made moonshine with. They'd been lucky they hadn't poisoned themselves.

"Hey, Brendan," Quin said. "Come on up."

Brendan removed the hat from his head and scratched behind his ear. "Why don't you come down?"

" 'Fraid you might fall out?" asked Quin as he lumbered down the rope ladder.

"Afraid I might break the ladder."

He had to be at least six-foot-five, thought Quin, as he reached the ground and dismounted the ladder. Brendan had always been tall for his age, but never more so than now. He looked extremely intimidating in that uniform.

If the two of them hadn't known each other since they were toddlers, Quin would have given the gentle giant a larger berth. As it was, though, he slapped Brendan resoundingly on the back.

"What brings you over here?"

"I got a call." Brendan looked a little uncomfortable. He nodded toward Stella's house. "Seems there's a prowler around here. Something about trespassing on private property."

It took Quin a second or two, but then he realized Stella had to have phoned about him being in her tree house. "Women."

"You said it. I'm taking you into custody." Brendan grinned. "You can buy me a beer at the Littlemouth Tavern."

"Aren't you on duty?"

"Not really." Brendan shrugged. "Stella insisted I put my uniform on when I came to arrest you. Seemed amusing at the time."

"Hilarious." Quin shot an annoyed glance toward Stella's back door, figuring she was watching. "Aren't you going to cuff me?"

"Nah, you're not resisting."

"Yeah, but it might make Stella feel guilty."

"I highly doubt it, Quin. With the mood she's in, she'd probably insist I give her my keys."

That put all the wrong sorts of images in Quin's head. He was already a prisoner of Stella's love. "Let's go get that beer."

"My cruiser's out front."

As they left the yard, Quin yelled at Stella's back door, "I'll be back."

Quin shoved his socks into his suitcase, using them to cushion the few breakables he carried while traveling. The phone call to his editor, Mark, had gone well, better than he'd expected. With any luck at all, he'd be out of Littlemouth by the next day, and out of the country by the following. Mark had said he'd call ASAP with an assignment and flight information.

That had been several hours ago. He'd spent a week thinking about where he'd gone wrong with Stella, hoping she'd answer his phone calls, or talk things over with him. It was as if she'd disappeared from the face of Littlemouth. Not even Prissy would tell him where she was.

Other than Brendan, the whole town had closed ranks against him, as if he'd done something to deliberately hurt one of their own. He couldn't see how he'd said or done anything to hurt Stella. Hadn't he asked her to come with him?

Finally he'd come to the conclusion that a relationship between them simply wasn't meant to be. His status as Littlemouth's bad boy and least-favored citizen had been reinstated, making the town anything but welcoming. So he'd placed that call to Mark.

Checking the bedside clock, he saw it was already eleven P.M., probably too late to hear from Mark again tonight.

Quin was antsy, restless. He needed to escape. Pacing around the room he'd lived in for most of his childhood, the urge to escape became too strong for him to deny. He'd take a walk, clear the cobwebs from his brain, tie the loose ends time in Littlemouth had left him with.

The class reunion was scheduled for the following night. He wanted to be far, far away before then. He didn't want to relive what he'd gone through ten years earlier, watching Stella from a distance and knowing she could never belong to him and he could never belong in Littlemouth.

Nothing had changed except he'd learned a tough lesson. You can't go back.

He'd go see Tramp, go visit the tree house. He might never see either of them again. He wasn't going to say goodbye to Stella. Clearly, she'd already said her farewells that day when she'd shattered his heart. But maybe, in the safety of the tree house, he could lay to rest the ghosts of their childhood, give up the fantasy of her he'd been clinging to.

Yeah, that was the ticket. He was going to dispel some ghosts.

Quin shrugged. It wasn't so awful being an adventurer, knowing the next day could bring a new wonder, a new adventure. It wasn't a bad life at all.

It would have been fun, though, to share it with someone he loved. Someone he found more exciting than any place he'd ever visited, more awe-inspiring than any shining star.

Stella had an absolutely horrid week. Other than leaving her house to attend school, she lived life like a prisoner. Quin called so frequently, she'd taken to leaving the phone off the hook. She barricaded herself in the house behind deadbolt locks. Although she'd allowed her mother in to check on her when her worry became evident, otherwise she hadn't let anyone else in the house.

She wanted to be left alone. To suffer in private. To figure out where and how she was supposed to go from here.

The last thing she wanted to do was see Quin. It was great that Brendan had so easily been able to run him off. Great. Really. She was glad Quin was gone. Good riddance to bad rubbish. Truly.

It was time to stop trying to fool herself. She felt as though one of her limbs had been loped off.

Tramp suffered as badly as she did. He layed by the front door and whimpered for Quin. She'd been tempted to join him and do the same. Somehow the two of them managed to bond with each other and derive comfort from their shared loss.

Tonight, Stella couldn't face going upstairs to her lonely bedroom, so she'd bundled up her pillows and a quilt to camp out on the living room sofa. Tramp sat on the floor beneath her feet, with sad brown eyes fixed on the front door.

"Face it, pup. We've been abandoned."

Tramp lifted his head, listening. Unexpectedly, he leaped to his feet and ran through the kitchen to the back door. Upon reaching it, he leaned his head back and howled, sending quivers down Stella's spine because he sounded exactly like a lonely wolf.

"What is it, boy?"

Tramp scratched at the door. Stepping into her house slippers and then donning her bathrobe, Stella hurried to join the dog. When she flipped the switch, the back yard flooded with light. Immediately before her eyes, caught in mid-climb on the rope ladder, was the abandoner in question. What was he doing here this late at night?

Some part of her, the part she tried to tamp down out of sight, was thrilled Brendan hadn't managed to run Quin off after all.

Once the light came on, Quin froze a moment and then descended the ladder. He looked good, almost too good, wearing his trademark leather bomber jacket and tight jeans. When she opened the back door, both she and Tramp went out to discover what had brought him.

The night was starlit and unseasonably warm, with the barest hint of a breeze stirring the leaves on the oak tree. Stella's vision adjusted to the dark as Quin stalked toward her. She took a step back, then forced courage through her limbs and a smile on her face. "Hi."

"Before you call Brendan on me again, I think I should warn you I came to say good-bye."

"You're leaving? So soon?" Her lungs felt as though all the air had been squeezed from her.

"I expect to fly out of here tomorrow afternoon at latest."

"So you'll miss the reunion."

"Looks that way."

How did he have the ability, standing at least fifteen feet away from her, to make her palms damp, her heart pound, and her stomach plummet? Balling her hands so tightly her nails bit into the tender skin, she forced herself not to run into his arms.

Tramp sat at his feet, lifting one paw, begging Quin for attention, and she was determined not to be so desperate for his affections.

He was really leaving. Without her. Turning away so he couldn't see, she brushed back a tear. His leaving would hurt that much more if he knew how she felt.

Why couldn't he get it? Why couldn't he understand she needed him to love her enough to risk everything? "What's out there for you, Quin, that you haven't found yet?" she asked him softly.

"I expect I'll know it when I find it." He shrugged and thought about how beautiful Stella was, draped in moonlight with her hair tangled by the breeze. She stood near the light and he could make out a crinkle on her face where she'd been lying on it, probably sound asleep. "I didn't mean to wake you."

"You didn't." She exhaled a drawn-out sigh and he ached with the need to capture it between his lips.

There was no point in it, though. Her answer had been clear when she'd turned away after he'd asked her to come with him. "I'd better be going."

"Wait. What's in your pocket?"

He felt a little sheepish as he pulled out a small glass salt shaker. "I'd planned a little slug hunting."

Stella smiled, but didn't say anything.

"Well, so long," he said as he headed toward the gate.

She grabbed his arm to prevent him from leaving. She asked, "Are you coming back? Ever?"

"Sure," he said, not meaning it at all. "I'll be seeing you around." Shaking off her arm, he left.

Stella was left standing there, she and Tramp, tears falling freely now. She hadn't believed a word he'd said. Quin wasn't ever coming home to her again.

A sharp pain seized her chest, making it nearly impossible to breathe, like she'd been caught up in a vice. She couldn't believe she was just letting him walk away from her.

Quin had proven that he loved her by inviting her to come along with him. Why had it taken his leaving for her to realize that?

Minutes flew past and then she realized he hadn't left at all. Or if he had, he'd turned back around. He stood silently by the gate as if waiting for her to invite him in.

Could she? Should she? If they talked it out, could she bring him to see her side of things? If that failed, at least she'd have a few extra moments of his time. "Come in with us, Quin."

Nodding, he followed Tramp and her into the house and settled himself at the kitchen table.

"I'll make some tea," she said, then scurried about nervously putting the kettle on to boil. She didn't much think he liked the stuff, but he hadn't demurred. If he'd declined, she'd probably have asked him to go hunt slugs with her again. Anything to keep him here a little longer.

Placing a bowl of freshly baked cookies on the table, she then plunked herself down across from him and blushed, remembering how she'd blatantly seated herself so close beside him the last time he'd sat in that chair.

He reached out and stroked the back of her hand lightly with his fingertip. "I'm going to miss you."

"I'll miss you too. I know I should have called you back before now, but I needed time to—" The kettle whistled.

She jumped as if she'd been burnt by hot coals. But it wasn't the kettle that startled her. It was the way she'd reflexively responded to his touch. "I'll get our tea."

"If you think you've been saved by the bell," Quin said with a shadow of a smile on his face, "you can think again."

"I know." After quickly filling mugs with steaming water, she popped a tea bag in each, then brought them back to the table.

Dunking her tea bag up and down in the water, she kept her gaze directed away from Quin. She couldn't meet his eyes when she said what she simply had to say before he left her life forever. "I love my life here. I love teaching school. I love this house. I love the continuity of a small community where I've known my neighbors forever and they me. But Quin—"

She looked up and was swept away in his gaze. Love, laughter, and longing, everything she ever thought she needed from a man was all to be found right there in the way he looked at her. "But Quin, I also love you."

He abruptly stood, his chair back slapping against the wainscoting behind him. Then he began pacing like a caged panther again and she wanted to reach out to him, pull him to her bosom to comfort him. She didn't know how.

So she stood and pulled his hand into hers. "It wouldn't be fair for me to lock you away where you don't belong, any more than it would be fair for me to abandon the life I worked so hard to create for myself—where I belong. Can't you see that? Either way, the cost for each of us would be too great."

Silence filled the room, not even the sound of his gentle breathing reached her ears.

Dropping his hand, she again took her seat at the table, and lowered her head into her palms. "That's what I couldn't say when you asked me to go with you. I'm sorry."

"I'm sorry, too, Stell," he replied, running a hand through her hair in a gesture of understanding.

When she finally raised her head, she looked around to find he was gone. She wondered if he'd ever really been there at all.

Chapter Fourteen

"This emergency meeting of TROUBLE is called to order," said Cait Boswell early the next morning. She steadily met the gaze of each woman seated in her tidy living room, with the exception of Prissy who'd buried herself in a handkerchief. Loud sniffles and sobs could be heard coming from her, not the least muffled by the bit of lace in her hands.

Cait continued, "We need to discuss our matchmaking plan to make Stella Quin's bride."

"More like bride-less, if you ask me," muttered Janice dryly. "We've fouled up somewhere, ladies."

Prissy moaned shrilly. "My daughter refuses to leave her house except to go to work and return.

164

She won't even—*sob*—work in her garden any-more."

"Enough dramatics, Priss," replied Cait. "Be quiet and maybe we can figure a way out of this mess."

Debby took a swig of her smoothie, then shook her head. "Can't make him love her, you know."

"But he does," was Miss Tipplemouse's calm reply. "He simply hasn't sorted it out yet."

"What makes you so certain?" asked Prissy.

"Believe me, if any young man had looked at me the way Quinlan looks at Stella, I wouldn't be single right now." Miss Tipplemouse sighed vol-ubly.

"I suppose it's possible," said Debby with a wrinkled brow. "He reminds me so much of his father. He always was a stubborn and slow man. I had to nearly hit him over the head to get him to propose."

"So what should we do?" asked Prissy, wiping the tears from her eyes.

"I propose we tell him," Cait smiled a wicked smile, "the truth."

Each of the other women abandoned their chairs and stood in unison. "The truth?!"

Prissy's forehead wrinkled. "But if we tell them we engineered everything, won't they be, clunk me over the head if I'm wrong, furious?"

Janice snorted. "Of course they will."

"I didn't say we'd tell them everything," Cait replied. "Just the truth. Some of it."

"Don't think of it that way," Quin said into the phone receiver. "Think of it as gaining the best editor you ever had."

As he hung up from the call to his boss, another caller beeped in.

"Quinlan," said his mother in a breathless voice. "The bike has broken down again. I'm at Cait's. Pick me up?"

"I've got one stop to make on the way, but I should be there within half an hour," he replied. Disconnecting the call, he then went in search of his shoes and ultimately found them in the family room cauldron. He didn't even take the time to wonder how, or why, they were in there before he placed them on his feet and headed out.

Stepping from the shower, Stella took one look at her reflection in the mirror above the sink, and dashed right back into the tub. No amount of water was going to wash away the bags beneath her eyes. She and Tramp had been up all night.

Around four in the morning, she'd reached a conclusion. Whether Quin loved her equally well or not, she loved him enough for both of them.

With the right mind set, she was certain she could learn to enjoy traveling. To like living out of a suitcase. There were many benefits to traveling, like museums, and castles, and jungles, and well, lots of things. Like hairy spiders, mosquitos, wild animals, and poisonous snakes. Not to mention bandits, criminals, and drug lords. But they weren't important because, most importantly of all, she'd be with Quin.

There was no way she was going to let him set foot outside Littlemouth without her by his side. Even if she had to grovel. Groveling would probably be good for her.

All she had to do was leave the shower, get dressed, grab the suitcase she'd packed that morning and head over to his house.

Leaving the shower was the problem.

Her face looked like she hadn't slept, which was true. She hadn't. He'd probably take one look at her and change his mind. Darn, darn, double darn. She had to do it and do it fast. No telling when he'd depart for Wichita and his flight back east.

Forcing herself to emerge from the tub, she kept her eyes on the floor to avoid her image in the mirror and made a dash for her bedroom. She could be dressed and at his house within half an hour.

When she arrived at the Gregory's, she grabbed Tramp's leash in one hand and a suitcase in the other and waggled it to the door while Tramp's tail wagged in excitement. Settling the suitcase on the porch, she tapped a swift rap on the etched-glass door. A man's silhouette appeared and her heart began doing flip-flops. Soon now, she'd know one way or the other how Quin felt about her, about them.

When the door opened, though, she was disappointed. She hadn't expected Quin's dad to answer. "Hi. Is Quin home?"

Her voice came out raspy, reedy, but he didn't seem to notice. "Sorry, Stella. You just missed him."

"I missed him?" She wasn't going to cry and she wasn't going to give up. If she had to, she'd chase him all the way to Hong Kong. "How long ago did he leave?"

He consulted his watch. "About fifteen, twenty minutes."

"Do you know where he went?"

"To the airport."

"I mean where he's flying to?"

"I think he said New York."

Stella bit her upper lip. She'd missed Quin, all because she couldn't face her own image and get out of the blasted shower. Taking a deep breath, she stiffened her spine. She'd just head for the Big Apple. Surely she could find him in a sea of what, seven million people?

"Do you have an address for him?"

"Maybe you could come back later and ask Debby. She's got all his information."

His answer filled her with depression. She was a total fool. Once she controlled her emotions, she caught Mayor Gregory eyeing her suitcase and realized how bad it looked. She couldn't bear the idea of the whole town pitying her. It had been bad enough after her broken engagement. She couldn't take it again, not when she felt so lost and splintered.

"I'd appreciate it if you wouldn't tell anyone I was here. Okay?"

Giving her a kind smile, he replied, "Mum's the word."

Mayor Gregory was not the gossip his wife was and she knew she could trust his word. With as much dignity as she could muster, she murmured her thanks, then walked Tramp back to the car.

Feeling as if she'd been knocked down by a wrecking ball, she slowly drove toward home. Tramp whined, then settled down on the passenger seat.

He'd left. Quin had left her behind.

An idea came to her. It was probably absurd, but it was a chance. Turning the corner with both hands on the wheel, the car came up on two wheels then came back to earth with a thud. There was a chance she could catch him at the airport.

Roaring onto Cait's street, she stomped on the

brake with both feet making the tires screech in protest. Was that Quin's rental car parked in front of Cait's home? Maybe he'd stopped there first to say farewell?

Stella sent up a silent prayer of thanks, then threw the car into park, heedless of the fact it was in the middle of the street blocking traffic. Tramp followed her out of the car in a bound and they both dashed up to bang on Cait's door.

Once Cait opened the door and admitted Stella, she couldn't relax until she saw Quin's face. "Is he here?"

Cait, with a knowing smile, nodded. She led Stella and Tramp into the living room.

She saw him before she entered the room. He looked scrumptious. Her desperation lightened, as if ten tons had been lifted off her heart. He hadn't left.

"I'm glad you're here, Stella," he told her with a mischievous gleam in his eyes. "It seems we've been the victims of malicious gossip."

She looked at him, wondering what he was talking about, while Tramp jumped up on two legs and gave Quin a lick on the face. She resisted an urge to follow suit.

Quin told the dog to sit and gave him a pat. "It appears that TROUBLE, as well as each of us, has been had."

"We've been had?" Stella twisted her hands,

wanting to drag him out of there so she could throw herself at him in relative privacy.

"I take it you aren't the best-selling novelist, Constance Howard, are you?"

"No." What on earth was he talking about? Couldn't he tell that she wanted to get him alone? She held up her thumb and pointed to the door with it, but Quin ignored her gesture.

"You've never heard of Doc Danger?"

"Is he the guy you asked me about before?"

Quin nodded.

"He's a total mystery to me." Again she gestured that she wanted to talk with him, and again he ignored it.

"Here's the latest rumor—that you write the Home Gardener column for *Better Gardens*. Is that true?"

"Yes, it's true. Quin, I want to talk with you—"

"You don't work for the government doing top-secret scientific research?"

She shook her head. He was going somewhere with this and Stella only wished she knew what he was trying to say because all she could think about was throwing her arms around him. She really didn't want to do it in front of an audience, but if he didn't hurry up and take the hint, she'd throw caution, and herself, to the wind.

"And you didn't catch Poindexter in your wedding veil?"

"Good heavens, no!"

"It appears you're right, Cait," he said, turning to address her. "Whoever has been doing this gossiping must be stopped."

The Troublemakers began to chatter simultaneously while Quin winked at Stella over their heads. She wasn't quite clear about what had been going on, but she was relieved to have missed it. Now all she had to do was tell him she'd die if he left without her.

"When's your flight leave, Quin?" she asked in a voice loud enough to be heard over the din.

Everyone grew silent and waited for his answer.

"I can't get away as quickly as I'd thought," he replied. "I've got a couple of loose ends to wrap up."

And then the smile he gave her sent the blood coursing through her veins faster than any speeding bullet. It was going to be okay. He still loved her. That was all she needed to know.

"Okay. Will I see you later?"

"You bet. I'll be over around five o'clock or so?"

Stella smiled. "Fine. Tramp and I'll be waiting for you."

With a light step, she left Cait's house to find Brendan McCade's patrol car parked behind hers in the middle of the street. "I'm moving it now,

Brendan," she cried as she dashed to her vehicle, Tramp running along with her.

Brendan grinned. "Wouldn't have given you a ticket, anyway. Just get it out of the street."

"Thanks!" Stella waved at him as soon as she and Tramp were seated. She pulled off down the street. Suddenly life didn't seem quite so dismal as it had that morning. Turning the rearview mirror so she could look at her reflection, she decided she looked darn good in bags.

As soon as Stella left, the women descended on Quin like buzzards, but he was getting used to it. They didn't intimidate him at all this time.

"But what about the reunion?" asked Cait. "It's tonight, you know."

Quin gave her a reassuring smile. "This time, I'm certain I've got it covered."

Five o'clock seemed to take forever to roll around. Stella gave up pacing and had taken to brushing Tramp for as long as he'd sit still for it.

Fortunately, the hellhound seemed to like being brushed. Also fortunate, some of his hair had begun coming back in, leaving him looking a bit less like pink scar tissue and more like a lapdog with five o'clock shadow.

Promptly at five, Tramp rushed to the front door and Stella sprinted behind him. When she threw open the door, Quin stood there with an irresistible slug slime grin on his face and she knew instantly he was up to mischief. He held two brown paper grocery bags in his tuxedo-clad arms.

She'd totally forgotten! The reunion was tonight.

Handing her one of the bags, he knelt to give Tramp a head scratch, then came in the house treading perkiness and cheer behind him. Stella narrowed her eyes at him. He was definitely up to something.

Tagging along behind them, she closed the door, then peeked into the sack. It looked as if all it contained was wadded up clothing. "What are you up to?"

With twinkling eyes, he dropped his bag on the kitchen table and began unloading it. "I brought you something, Stell."

Looking at the wad of shirts in his arms, she was totally nonplused. "Dirty clothing?"

"Yeah, gossip has it you like doing laundry." The twinkle in his eyes became a loving caress. Pulling a small white box with red lettering from the bottom of the sack, he handed it to her.

Slug Slammer: Slams Snails Dead. "Oh, Quin. You shouldn't have!" She felt all warm and glowy inside. The man had to love her if he was worried about the slugs in her garden.

"The laundry's for you too," he said. "I have to warn you, though, about some of my bad habits."

Stella leaned back against the door frame, waiting for him to go on, *Slug Slammer* in one of her hands and the other still holding his second paper sack. When he was in one of these moods, she knew she couldn't rush him. "I thought you were perfect. You can't seriously mean you have *any* bad habits?"

"I sometimes forget to put my dirty clothes in the laundry bag. I've been known to drop wet towels on my bed. And worst of all, according to my mother, I forget to empty my pockets."

What was he trying to tell her?

He sighed ruefully as he nodded toward the sack she still held in her arms. "You'll have to look through each and every pocket before loading those in the washer, I'm afraid."

He was telling her to look through his pockets. Stella poured the bag of clothing onto the kitchen table and frantically patted each item until at last she felt something in one of the jeans pockets. Reaching her hand in, her fingers closed on a small, velvety box. A ring box?

She couldn't move. Couldn't bring herself to pull it out of the pocket. A tear dripped down her face and Quin took a step nearer to her, then another step, until he bundled her into his arms.

She couldn't stop the downpour now but he held

her tightly making soft comforting noises and rubbing her hair and the back of her head.

"I'm going to ruin your tux."

Quin shrugged. "It's a rental. Aren't you going to open the box?"

Stella shook her head. "I don't think I can."

Quin released her long enough to slide the box from beneath her shaking fingers. Pulling back the lid, he revealed the most perfect diamond ring she'd ever seen in her life.

"If this means you want to marry me, Quin," Stella said between sobs, "the answer is yes. I'll go anywhere you want me to, just as long as you let me stay right by your side."

"Oh, Stella." He pulled her tightly into his arms as if he'd never let her go. "I've got some news to share with you. I hope you won't be disappointed if we have to delay that travel I promised you."

"Delay?"

"I talked with my boss. You're holding the new editor of the Midwest region of the magazine. Other than the very rare assignment, I don't have to leave Littlemouth."

"And when you do, I'll be right by your side. I want to see the world through your eyes."

"I love you, Stella. Wherever you are, there's always excitement. You're my home." Quin slipped the ring over her finger where it sparkled as brightly as the love in his eyes. "And best of all . . ."

She placed her palm over the acorn hanging from his neck. "There's no place like home?"

"No, Stella." He laughed. "Best of all, since we're engaged, now you'll have to go to the reunion with me. The whole town would be up in arms otherwise."

Stella grabbed the dirty clothes off the table and threw them over his head. "I'll go change. Don't you dare leave without me."

Epilogue

It was a perfect day for a wedding. The weather had cooperated, with endless blue skies and only a few white wispy clouds flittering across the wide Kansas panorama. The temperature was warm without being hot, breezy without being windy. Absolute perfection, in fact.

For the Troublemakers, Mother's Day was an especially important event. Celebrating it with a wedding made it even more perfect.

Stella's yard had been beautifully decorated. All the flowers she'd planted were in bloom and Prissy had added a profusion of yellow carnations anywhere she could find a vacant spot. Bright lemon-hued bows had been tied on each of the rental chairs lined up in a row facing the huge old oak tree.

A stark white canopy covered a small dais where the groom anxiously awaited his bride. Three musicians sat near the back door playing chamber music on their stringed instruments.

Brendan McCade, looking as good in a tuxedo as he did in uniform, had agreed to serve as usher. He'd only been a little nonplused when the Troublemakers insisted upon sitting together on the front row of chairs.

At the rear of the yard, numerous tables had been covered in green and yellow linen, and they sported both a gaiety of flowers along with the bounteous supply of food catered by the Little Mouth Diner.

A huge white wedding cake teetered on a table by itself. In addition to the traditional bride and groom perched on the top tier, a small figurine of a dog had been added as well.

Several punch bowls were filled with frothy concoctions and crystal cups were stacked and ready. Another table was covered with champagne flutes and uncorked bottles of the beverage.

It looked as if the whole town of Littlemouth had turned up to wish Stella and Quin happy. Even The Gargoyle had come with a perky smile on her face.

Everything was perfect.

All except one thing, that is.

The Troublemakers, huddled together upon the front row, were sobbing their hearts out. Loudly.

"It's so romantic," sniffled Miss Tipplemouse.

"Oh, it is," cried Cait, wailing loudest of them all. Her normally steel-like bosom quaked with each of her indrawn breaths.

"They're going to be so happy," sobbed Janice sentimentally.

Prissy sighed. "Our plan came off perfectly, didn't it?"

Debby, without a high-protein smoothie in her hands for once, was so emotional she couldn't speak at all. Her son wouldn't be going away again. What more could a mother ask for, especially on Mother's Day?

A hush came over everyone as the music changed beat. Tramp exited the house, his collar and leash decorated with a rope of flowers, led by Ian Andrews. The dog carried a straw basket of rose petals in his mouth. As Ian led him along the yellow carpeting which had been laid down as a path to the canopy, rose petals were haphazardly strewn all over the yard.

Everyone began to clap in delight at Tramp's cheerful participation. Yanking against his lead, he dashed all-out for Quin, dragging Ian behind him.

Next Anne emerged, dressed in emerald silk,

and looking as lovely as any flower in Stella's glorious garden.

"I was so afraid," said Prissy, as Anne joined Quin in awaiting Stella, "that the wedding would have to be postponed."

"Postponed?" cried Cait in a shocked voice.

Prissy nodded. "Wait until you see it. Stella insisted upon making her own gown. It took hours to sew."

"She couldn't find anything at the wedding shop in Wichita?"

"They had some gorgeous gowns, but none of them would do." Prissy's brow furrowed.

"Well, I'll be," declared Debby.

"Bridal nerves." Miss Tipplemouse nodded reassuringly. "Affects most brides, I've read. No telling how a young woman will react when it comes her time to unite with her one true love."

The musicians began to play the wedding march. Everyone rose from their seats to get a glimpse of the bride. Quin's father was bestman, and Stella was led down the aisle by her father.

Anyone who hadn't known otherwise, would have sworn her wedding dress had been fashioned by a designer. Beading and lace covered the bodice, while the skirt was tapered with flowing flounces trimmed with matching lace and beads.

On her head she wore a tiara, and flowers and beads had been woven throughout her hair, which she wore down in a soft cloud around her shoulders.

Quin had never seen a more beautiful woman. Their eyes met, locked. The nearer she came, the larger his smile became, until she was there, having her hand placed in his by her father.

Laughing, they both turned toward the minister, but then turned back to the guests when a series of cheers and applause went up. Quin held up his hand, joined with Stella's, in a victory salute.

It didn't quiet everyone down though, until Stella pulled white roses from the bouquet she carried. Cait had made the arrangement, centered around a white gingerbread birdhouse. She hadn't been aware of Stella's inclusion of five perfect white roses, though.

Quin and Stella walked together to Prissy's side. After Stella handed her a white rose, they each bent to give her a kiss. Next, they gave a rose to Debby, who subsided in a series of elated sniffles. Then they gave a rose and kisses to each of the other members of the outrageous readers group.

Finally, they turned and rejoined the Mayor, Anne, Ian, Tramp, and the minister to receive their wedding vows.

Tears of happiness coursed down Stella's glowing face and Quin had to bite his lip to keep from doing the same.

The Troublemakers hugged each other as the

couple recited the words that would bond them together in a lifetime of happiness.

"We do good work, don't we?" said Prissy.

"Oh yes," sighed Miss Tipplemouse. "Our plan was a resounding success. Each of our goals was met right on deadline."

As Stella and Quin kissed to celebrate their union, Janice's gaze wandered, then fixed on Brendan and Cait's unmarried daughter, Anne. She murmured, "Maybe we should consider playing cupid again?"

"I'm so happy," Stella said, joy erupting inside her. Everything she'd ever wanted was coming true. The man of her dreams and her heart had at last come home to stay.

"You're going to be happier still," replied Quin as he kissed the tip of her nose. "Tonight you get to play Jane to my Tarzan. Our tree house awaits."

11/4/03

11/4/03